The Lady and Her Secret

Ruth A. Casie

The Lady and Her Secret

Timeless Scribes
Publishing

Timeless Scribes Publishing LLC

Digital ISBN-13: 978-1-945679-95-7
Print ISBN-13: 978-1-945679-96-4

Editor: The Editing Hall - Chris Hall
Cover Artist: Wicked Smart Designs

This edition published by arrangement with Timeless Scribes Publishing LLC.

www.TimelessScribes.com

Also by Ruth A. Casie

Regency Romance
THE LADIES OF SOMMER-BY-THE-SEA
The Lady and Her Quill
The Lady and the Spy
The Lady and Her Duke
The Duke's Lost Love
RETURN TO THE LADIES OF SOMMER-BY-THE-SEA
The Lady and the Barrister
The Lady and the Earl
The Lady and the Rogue
The Lady and Her Secret

♥ ♥ ♥

Fantasy Romance
THE STELTON LEGACY
The Guardian's Witch
The Highlander's English Woman
The Maxwell Ghost

Crossover Series - Pirate Romance
PIRATES OF BRITANNIA
Donald (Sons of Sagamore)
Hugh (Sons of Sagamore)
Graham (Sons of Sagamore)
The Pirate's Jewel
The Pirate's Redemption

♥ ♥ ♥

Also by Ruth A. Casie

Time Travel Romance
THE DRUID KNIGHT SERIES
Knight of Runes
Knight of Rapture
The Red Slippers — A Short Story
The Druid Knight Tale I — A Short Story—Expanded
The Druid Knight Tale II — A Short Story

♥ ♥ ♥

Contemporary Novellas
HAVENPORT
Happily Ever After
The Witching Hour
Never Say Never
Echoes of Betrayal
How to Marry a Stuart Brother
Heart of the Matter

♥ ♥ ♥

Boxed Sets
NIGHT OF LYONS
The Lady and the Lyon's Scandal
THE LIGHT OF LOVE
The Lady and the Flame
CHRISTMASTIDE KISSES
The Lady and the Christmas Brooch

♥ ♥ ♥

Chapter One

October 1829
Sommer-by-the-Sea, England

Lady Rachel Emerson drew her treasured brown shawl close and fisted the wool at her neck to block out the damp mist from stealing what little warmth she had. Foolish, that's what she was. Who in their right mind goes out at eight o'clock in the morning on a Northern England beach road in late October? Really? No one would describe her as compulsive, but what else could explain her uncontrollable urge to come here? Now. Before the house was gone and nothing was left.

Rachel reached into her pocket and pulled out a folded, tattered note once again. If she read it once, she read it a hundred times. *Meet me tonight.* R. She put the unsent note away and continued on her way.

A breeze teased the tendrils of Rachel's long, raven-black hair, releasing them from the chignon at the nape of her neck. The striking contrast of her dark tresses against her fair, porcelain-like complexion created an undeniable aura of ethereal beauty.

Slender and graceful, Rachel was much more than a beautiful woman. It took only one glance at her mesmerizing azure eyes to see her keen intelligence and authenticity and why people were drawn to her.

She made her way down Coach Road, where the road split in three directions. There, she was greeted by the village sign, *Sommer-by-the-Sea.* Against the setting of an overcast sky, fingers of fog roiled at the sign's base and made it appear as if it hung in midair.

She glanced down the middle road, Queen's Promenade, and then the road to the right, King's Way. Both were grand names from a different time when royalty once inhabited the Sommer-by-the-Sea Castle. It had been over a century since the last royal occupant. Queen's Promenade skirted the edge of Baycliff Forest with evergreens that thinned and gave way to the trimmed and shaped grounds of the grand manors near the beach.

Rachel let out a breath as she glanced to the right, King's Way. This road led directly into the village and was almost wide enough for two wagons. Rather than move on, she remained fixed in place, listening to the cadence of crashing waves in the distance, creating a familiar, soothing rhythm. The breeze picked up and sent sand and dust up the road from the beach. She shivered and pulled her shawl closer. For a moment, she regretted starting her journey so early in the morning.

"My own fault," Rachel muttered, "for putting this visit off." At midnight, the Historical Society would take ownership of the estate property and its contents. She had to be gone by then. Nothing like leaving things to the last minute.

Today was her last chance to walk through Emerson Manor and find what she lost a long time ago. It was precious to her then and even more so now. Deep down, the comfort of home called to her. Finding that feeling again warmed her soul. Finding anything else would be a miracle.

"Come on, Rachel, one foot in front of the other," she said to no one.

She squinted down Queen's Promenade. Visibility was poor. There wasn't any way anyone could make out the cemetery a quarter mile away—or the entrance to Emerson Manor on the hill a mile past that—not with this mist.

As a seasoned village resident, she knew the watery morning sun struggling through the clouds would make it difficult for the haze to clear.

Another look at the gathering mist sent a chill up her back. Rachel rubbed her arms, unable to be soothed. *Easy. Stay calm.* She cast a quick glance from the short shrubs at the edge of the road to the thickening mist around her. Anyone could hide in this fog, and she wouldn't know until they stood nose to nose.

"Breathe. Nothing's there. It's your overactive imagination."

The tall grass twitched. Rachel's chest pounded. She dared not make a sudden move. She sniffed the air and caught the tangy odor of brine, seaweed, and mucky sand. Another sniff. Some people were concerned about the foxes that roamed the area. Not Rachel. It was skunks that terrified her ever since she was five.

"Dear Lord, Rachel, what were you thinking?" Her father's voice had a nasal twang, probably caused by the handkerchief he held to his nose.

"I wanted to pet Brenna's kitty. It was a gift from her uncle. He brought them back from his voyage to America."

"I thought as much." Her mother sounded annoyed. "Who gave you the kitty to pet? Brenna?"

"Yes. A boy kitty and a girl kitty." Rachel turned to her father. "I asked first, and Brenna said yes. Why are we going to the boathouse now? Doesn't the party start soon?"

"I'm telling you, Edythe. That Hutchington girl will come to no good."

"She is just a child, playing children's games." Her mother gave her a big smile and then turned back to her father. *"They will be the best of friends. You'll see."*

"At Rachel's expense." Father wagged his head. He didn't believe Mother for a moment. Still walking toward the dock, he glanced at her.

"You'll have to be brave, my little princess." His words were somber, but his eyes twinkled as they reached the water. In minutes, he had a fire blazing in the pit, and Mother had supplies on the outdoor table.

"Brave?" Rachel asked.

"Yes." Her mother pulled off her costume and gave it to Father.

"My costume," she cried, reaching for it. Shiny beads covered her beautiful costume and made it twinkle in the firelight. *"You don't let anyone into the party without a costume."*

"Hmm… not in this costume. Unless you want to go as a very smelly fairy," her father said, holding the pungent mess at arm's length. Five-year-old Rachel watched in horror as he tossed it into the fire.

"Farewell, little princess and brave handkerchief." He ceremoniously tossed the handkerchief into the fire pit as well. *"Life is not always comfortable. There are also some unpleasant moments. Sometimes it's even stinky."*

"Oh, Father. Don't be silly," she said with a laugh. He always made her laugh.

"Thank goodness," her mother said, sniffing her like a puppy, making her laugh even more. *"I can't smell anything."*

"Can I be a witch like you, Mother?" Rachel glanced from her father to her mother.

"I'm not sure." Her father turned away from tending the fire and gave Rachel a thoughtful gaze. *"You have to be pretty special to be a witch like your mother."* He returned and raked the fire to ensure nothing remained of the costume or his handkerchief.

"Don't give her any ideas." A particular look passed between her parents. "You know Rachel must be at least six before I can teach her spells. I think the first one will be eliminating odors."

Her mother washed her down for good measure and wrapped her in a soft towel while her father put out the fire.

"We've completed our task," he announced. He sniffed around Rachel. "You smell sweet as a rose. I'm sure Janet will have something special for you to wear to the party."

"In the future, Rachel—"

"Edythe, she's learned her lesson" Her father turned toward her. "Haven't you... Hmm. I can't call you my fairy princess. How about... my little ballerina?" Her father picked her up. "I want you to have only happy ever afters. No matter their size or who says you can touch them, Rachel, wild animals are not safe. Promise me you won't go near them again."

"I promise, Father." He carried her back to the manor and brought her to her room, where Janet waited.

He put her down, and Rachel ran inside.

"Oh, Janet. You made me another costume." On her bed was a lilac gown with a fitted bodice with beads in a pretty pattern. It had short, puffed sleeves trimmed with lace and a flowing gauze skirt with silver embroidery that made the skirt sparkle. There were black ballet slippers, but her eyes went to the small glittery crown.

"I thought you would be a princess ballerina." Janet handed her the crown. "It completes your costume."

After that encounter, she had a healthy respect for Brenna's skunks. Especially when her friend got tired of the black and white creatures and let them out into the wild. The pair of skunks made their new home in an abandoned badger burrow at the base of the town sign.

Her father was just as happy. There were few people like him. Sheldon Emerson, the Duke of Harrington, was an imposing and dignified man. Handsome beyond doubt, his dark blue eyes were captivating, complementing the roguish charm of his wavy dark hair now streaked with silver, and a brilliant smile that charmed everyone. Unlike the fathers of her friends, the duke was a remarkable man. Embracing free-thinking and possessing an insatiable thirst for knowledge, he was always engrossed in a book, which he eagerly discussed at the dinner table, drawing even a young Rachel into the conversations.

His playful sense of humor and quick wit endeared him to all who met. While he fulfilled his duties as a responsible Duke and managed his affairs adeptly, his heart belonged to his beloved wife, Edythe, and to their precious daughter, Rachel.

Now, a grown Rachel took one step backward and another before turning and quickly marching toward town. Better to wait for the fog to lift so she could see what was in front of her before going to the manor.

"Coward," Rachel mumbled. "You didn't come this far to run away. Hush," she said, as if a self-reprimand would quiet her mind.

Rachel followed the double row of ruts cut deeply into the ground by the heavy carriages and wagons and trudged down King's Way into the village. She danced around the puddles and deep mud patches caused by the early-morning rain.

It would take her another thirty minutes to reach the village. By the time the buildings on the West Heath on the outskirts of town were in sight, the sun had made its way through the clouds and took the edge off the chill.

Rachel continued down King's Way, past the merchant quarter. It hadn't changed at all. It still was a community of hardworking people. Stone and brick houses with steep roofs and gabled fronts lined the streets. Carts stood in front of the houses. Clothes hung on the rope lines to dry. People hurried about doing their chores.

Rachel entered Westmore Commons and stopped at the village's public notice board. She smiled when she read the notice about Emerson Manor and the Historical Society. The announcement was one among many others: a farm to be let, a position open at one of the clothiers in the village, the availability of gentlemen's and ladies' undergarments, an advertisement for fine writing papers, and another advertisement specifically to ladies—autumn novelties, an excellent way to identify whalebone stays. That made Rachel chuckle.

Rachel crossed the commons. Nannies were pushing carriages or sitting on benches chatting with each other. Other people hurried along, determined to reach their destination. She looked around at old landmarks, the castle and the church on the hill, Mrs. Bainbridge's Female Seminary, and the town hall opposite the village square. She headed toward the center of the commons.

The seasonal decorations made of leaves, gourds, and seasonal flowers dressed the town square and the business district and blanketed her with a comfortable sense of familiarity. The decorations may have been new, but they gave her a comforting feeling of home and helped her feel better about being away for so long.

The large white pavilion, built on a mound in the center of the town commons, provided a broad look of Sommer-by-the-Sea. Rachel climbed the steps, something she'd done hundreds of times for a view of the harbor. Masts swayed in the wind as the boats waited in the water.

Rachel let out a deep breath. Things looked familiar but were not the same. Places and people move on. Did she think they would stay the same for her? How foolish not to realize Sommer-by-the-Sea would change. She turned away from the harbor as if ignoring progress would make it stop and tried to swallow around the knot in her throat. What else had time changed?

From where she stood, she noticed new businesses were sprinkled among the old storefronts. The Tearoom occupied the far corner where the milliner used to be. Large flowerpots brimmed with bright yellow and red flowers and brown leaves in front of the shops created a festive look. Rich colors and trappings of autumn were all around. Yes, fall was her season. Sommer-by-the-Sea was her home.

"*Emerson Manor*," a voice whispered in her head. Half in anticipation and half in dread, she walked down the gazebo steps headed toward North Wickham Road and passed Mrs. Bainbridge's Female Seminary.

The aroma of freshly baked bread caught her attention. She imagined the taste of warm bread slathered with fresh butter—or better, raspberry jam—and she licked her lips. Her mother's baker, Anthony, made the best morning rolls and pastries. Anthony's father, Gaspar, was the village baker. She and Brenna stopped at his bakery almost every day after their classes at the seminary. Theirs was a slight diversion that went unnoticed as long as they brought Mrs. Bainbridge back a treat. Her mouth watered as she strolled down the street toward the Gordon and Langley Bookshop. Gaspar's Bakery was across the way, determined to satisfy her sweet tooth.

She stopped across from the bookshop, now called Dunston's Books. Disoriented, Rachel looked up and down the street. Rachel stood in the correct place. She searched for the large white building that housed Gaspar's bakery. It should be on the corner. She tilted her head as she stared at a pale-blue building with window boxes filled with bright yellow flowers. Yes. That was Gaspar's, but now the space was occupied by a modiste's shop.

She jumped at a soft, playful bark from a small dog that sniffed her feet. Before she could bend to pet the pup, the dog, an Aberdeen Terrier, rolled on its back, begging for a belly rub.

"MacDuff, what are you doing rolling around like that?" A woman approached the dog. "Come, we're off to the milliner. I need to get my hat for the masquerade ball."

"MacDuff. That's a wonderful name." Unable to resist the brindle coat, Rachel bent to pet the dog. MacDuff rolled on the ground, his tail beating the ground this puppy would melt anyone's heart. Masquerade ball? Had she heard the woman correctly? Her mother used to host one every year at the Manor.

The woman bent down and picked leaves off MacDuff's coat. "There, that's much better. Sorry, we have no time to play."

"That's all right," Rachel said, straightening. MacDuff went obediently and stood at the woman's feet but kept his eyes on her.

The woman went into the shop. MacDuff looked back and gave Rachel a soft woof.

"I'm sorry, too, but I have to go, as well."

She turned and crossed the street to get a better look at the bookshop window and stared at a poster.

The Duchess's Annual Masquerade Ball
October 30 at Emerson Manor
Nine to midnight (if you dare to stay to the witching hour)
Costume required.
Hosted by The Duke and Duchess of Harrington
The Women of Emerson Manor,
available at Victoria's Cottage

An arrow pointed to the right.

It would be wonderful to go to the ball. Rachel looked at the sign. *The Women of Emerson Manor.*

She glanced through the window at Victoria's Cottage and saw pots of creams, baskets of crystals, small packets of herbs, incense, and candles—a metaphysical shop. Edythe Emerson was a guest lecturer at The Seminary: *Magic, Witchcraft, and Religion* and *Witches, Myth, and Reality.* Her mother would enjoy this shop.

Rachel stepped inside. With her first breath, the familiar woodsy fragrance of bay, earthy mint, and the aromas of sage and rosemary greeted her. Other scents drew her farther into the shop. Lavender, honeysuckle, and rose mixed and created a floral bouquet of fragrances. She didn't stop; instead, she passed the lotions and jars and followed an overhead sign directing her to the rear of the shop. There she found a large empty table against the wall with a sign: *We regret that the book, The Women of Emerson Manor, is sold out.* But it was the picture next to the sign that caught her attention. She stared at a formal family portrait of her as a young girl with her mother and her grandmother.

A wave of loss rolled over her. She hadn't realized how much she wanted to hear her mother's voice, feel the touch of her hand, and snuggle into the warmth and safety of being home.

Her emotions gradually subsided until a sense of calm washed over her. Rachel turned to leave and stared into the eyes of a woman wearing a purple scarf.

"You'd better hurry if you're going to Emerson Manor," the woman said softly and turned to leave.

How did the woman know that was where she was going? What else did she know? With her emotions in turmoil, Rachel followed the woman out the door and looked everywhere. She found the street deserted in every direction but one. Rachel rushed toward the crowd of people by the town square.

Small groups, mostly women, congregated in a knot and chatted. Rachel walked through the crowd and searched for the purple scarf.

"May I have everyone's attention, please?" A woman holding papers commanded everyone's attention.

"Hush. Ina's speaking," someone called out. Rachel kept moving through the crowd as the group quieted. She fisted her hand and smashed it into her thigh. Had the woman with the purple scarf vanished into thin air?

"Thank you for your patience. The carriage to Emerson Manor will be here shortly."

Rachel spun around. Emerson Manor? Were these people all going there?

"We will be let off at the front door. When you arrive, go directly to the assignment table in the Great Hall. Today, it is just the finishing touches. You've all done a wonderful job of making this masquerade ball a success. Edythe Emerson would be proud."

"Ina, what about getting back into town?" someone in the crowd asked.

"That's a very good question." Ina rummaged through her papers. "The carriage will return promptly at three and bring us back here to the town square. That should give everyone plenty of time to get ready for the evening. Please remember to stay on the first floor when we get to the manor. We've closed the upper floors for this event. If there are no other questions, please get in line."

Rachel gave one last look at the crowd. She stood in the back of the line deciding the carriage ride was better to ride than walk to the manor.

The clattering noise of a large carriage grew louder as it approached. Finally, the old French Omnibus that the carriage maker, Mr. Wheeler, had in his shop pulled up. Once or twice a year, he dusted the large carriage off, harnessed the two-horse team, and took people for a ride. Now, the women filed in. She stood by, watching and searching for the woman with the purple scarf.

"Hurry, ladies," the groom called. Ina and a few latecomers took their seats. Rachel gave one last look for the woman and had to admit she wasn't anywhere to be found. Finally, Rachel entered the carriage and found a seat in the back.

Mr. Wheeler closed the door and pulled away.

The woman must have thought she was someone else.

Rachel was sure no one cared that she had returned. Going to Emerson Manor was purely voluntary, or was it?

Rachel gave the waterfront a last glance, then looked down the aisle.

She saw the profile of Brenna Hutchington.

Chapter Two

Suddenly seeing Brenna caught Rachel off guard. After all these years, the hurt should be gone. However, betrayal ran deep.

The Hutchingtons had a long history that went back fifteen generations to Richard Neville, the 16th Earl of Warwick, the King Maker. That the Hutchington name was held in high regard in Sommer-by-the-Sea was an understatement—they enjoyed a luminary status among the villagers. Not all family members handled that reputation well. Most were friendly and down-to-earth, but others abused their privilege and treated people cruelly.

Although Brenna's origins may not be noble, her pedigree was worthy of admiration. Her self-confidence was irresistible and drew people to her side. As a result of spending her time outdoors, her tanned complexion gave her a warm glow. She wore her medium-length brown hair gracefully, allowing it to cascade freely, framing her face. Yet, it was her deep-set brown eyes that give away the true Brenna. At times, they reflected her cunning nature, giving hints of a conniving and manipulative personality.

Rachel couldn't remember life without Brenna. Born days apart, their mothers, close friends themselves, bragged that the girls were friends and confidants from their days in the nursery. They were more like twin sisters than best friends. They did everything together. Even fell in love with the same boy, Pryce Somerset.

Pryce. She smiled. She was seventeen the day she met him.

The week before her mother's annual masquerade, on her way home from an afternoon of gathering seashells at the town beach, intent on getting her favorite pastry from Gaspar's, she carefully approached Water Street, ready to cross.

Water Street followed the coastline and was a series of winding curves that led to a straight section of the road as it came into Sommer-by-the-Sea. The last turn, which everyone called The Bend, was doubly dangerous, especially if you were in a carriage or wagon. A sharp curve and steep rise not only obscured anything coming toward you, but if you didn't slow down before the drop, well, the momentum carried you along, and you could quickly end up on the beach if the tide was out or, worse, underwater if the tide was in.

With nothing in sight, Rachel started to cross the road. Out of nowhere, she found herself the target of an oncoming carriage. Startled and incapable of making sense of what was happening, she froze.

"Whoa!" a deep male voice shouted. The horses drawing the phaeton squealed and reared, clawing their legs high above her. Finally, Rachel came to her senses and stumbled back, landing badly, her ankle giving way. She fell to the ground. The horses settled down inches away from her.

Someone jumped out from the carriage. Rachel looked up and stared at a pair of muscular legs. Rachel worked to catch her breath. With the sun glaring into her eyes, she didn't recognize who stood over her.

"God's teeth, I could have—Don't move. I'll take you to Dr. Manning." The rich, baritone voice was filled with surprise, concern, and urgency.

"Don't be silly. I'm fine." Rachel sat up, *straightening out her skirt. Her eyes traveled from his muscular legs up his almost bare, chiseled physique, revealing well-defined muscles that rippled beneath his skin. She quickly looked up further into his concerned eyes.* Who was he? *He helped her to her feet. She swallowed hard. Rachel had never seen a man's nearly bare chest before.*

"See." She took a step forward, and her leg buckled.

"God's teeth." He had fast reflexes. He caught her before she fell to the ground.

She held her head, light-headed from the pain in her ankle or overcome by seeing him with his shirt almost entirely open.

He easily held her as if she weighed nothing and didn't appear eager to put her down. His hazel eyes were striking, but his smile… took her breath away.

Rachel sniffed the air. "Skunk?"

"You can still smell it? The letter with instructions about where I was to go flew out of my hand. This black and white animal sprayed me when I stopped and picked it up."

"Don't tell me. You stopped at the fork in the road, King's Way and Queen's Promenade." She wanted to kiss that little skunk.

"Yes. How'd you know?"

"That little black and white animal and I are old friends. Did you give him the shirt off your back?"

He threw back his head and let out a peal of laughter. "No, I burned it on the side of the road. I was not fond of the smell. I'm Pryce Drake, er, the Earl Somerset. My family moved into Dyer Abbey. Let me take you home. It's the least I can do." *He placed her in the carriage's passenger seat. She glanced at him.*

"The Duke and Duchess of Ashworth have taken over the duchess's mother's property."

"Yes. My parents have recently moved into the Abbey."

"I'm Lady Rachel Emerson. We're practically neighbors, Lord Somerset." It was a toss-up. She couldn't decide if it was almost becoming another victim of The Bend or the handsome earl that caused

her heart to pound. Either way, she was surprised he couldn't hear it.

Standing tall, at least six feet, he commanded her attention. She had already stolen a glance at his open shirt. He had a sculpted athletic frame. His ebony-black hair cascaded in waves around his forehead, accentuating his hazel eyes that held her captive.

He had a neatly trimmed beard along his strong jawline, adding a hint of ruggedness to his otherwise refined appearance. And when he smiled, a contagious joy effortlessly tugged at her lips, coaxing her into sharing his warmth and creating an immediate connection between them.

Yes, she shamelessly exaggerated her injury to keep his attention.

Rachel's swift intake of breath amid the chatter in the carriage brought her back to the moment.

The carriage plodded along Manor Road, then turned at the Manor Road gate. Emerson Manor wasn't visible from the road. Once through the main gate, one had to drive a quarter of a mile up the knoll, then another quarter of a mile to the house. Everyone stopped at the top of the knoll for the dramatic effect as they did now. You were high enough to look down on the manor and the surrounding grounds from this vantage point.

Distinct gasps turned into soft conversations, and the carriage drove on.

Emerson Manor, last renovated in 1780 by her parents when they inherited the estate, stood large and imposing. The Emerson family's trade investments had done well. Not quite as well as those who lived in neighboring Newcastle upon Tyne with their coal, but well enough to informally affect events and developments of the thriving coastal village.

Other elite families soon joined the Emersons and created an exclusive enclave that gave the appearance of the aristocracy.

"Emerson Manor," Mr. Wheeler announced as he stopped in the circular drive and opened the carriage door. He helped the women down. "I'll be back at three. Don't be late, or you'll have a long walk back into the village."

The carriage emptied. Only two people remained, Brenna and Rachel.

Brenna was a Hutchington. In her mind, no one else mattered but her. She was conniving and manipulative and a master at it. Brenna got what she wanted, and Brenna wanted Pryce, but her trick didn't work. He had chosen Rachel. She remembered the evening clearly. She was sixteen.

Meet me tonight. P.

Rachel reread Pryce's note as she waited under the oak tree.

"Why the long face?" she asked as he approached her.

He ran his hand through his hair and paced in front of the tree.

Her bright mood evaporated. The more Pryce paced, the more he flexed his fists. He looked like a jockey bracing himself before a race. What could have made him so upset? He was doing well at Oxford. The younger son in the family, he'd secured a job as a solicitor at a prestigious investment company. All she could do was wait. A few more seconds passed.

"I know Brenna's your friend." He stopped pacing and looked at her. His eyes softened, and his body relented. "Rachel, I don't want to hurt you, but she's not your friend."

He told her everything.

"You are aware that Brenna will do anything to attract my attention. I've told her subtly and not so subtly that I am not interested. It appears she was still determined.

"She invited me to a surprise party for you and made me swear to secrecy. When I arrived, I found you weren't there or any other guests— only Brenna attempting to be alluring.

She never doubted Pryce's honor or truthfulness. Rachel knew Brenna all too well. Her little game didn't surprise her. That she would play her games at her best friend's expense, betray her… did leave her speechless. How often did Rachel console other friends because of

Brenna's disregard for their feelings? And the countless times she spent speaking to Brenna to make her understand what she'd done.

"You're going to believe him"—Brenna stood in front of her, arms crossed—"over me? You know, he's not your happy ever after."

"Why would he lie?" Rachel wanted Brenna to say it was a joke so they could go on being friends. Tell her it was a misunderstanding.

"You didn't invite anyone else to your 'party.' I asked. Only Pryce." Rachel's voice tightened as she struggled to keep it even and controlled.

Brenna's attention flittered from one place to another, any place other than on her. "Let's go to Gaspar's. He makes that pastry you can't stop eating, or we can go to the Tearoom."

She forgave Brenna for many things—never returning books, jewelry, her exaggerations and lies—but this wasn't easily ignored. "Why would you—"

"I didn't do anything. I would never do anything to hurt you," Brenna said, but her voice didn't convince Rachel. Her words sounded like a lie.

"Are you going to the Stewart gala tonight? I thought I'd wear my new gown. The one you like." Brenna flashed a smile, then turned away, and looked at the clock on the mantel in Rachel's room.

Betrayal flashed like a bolt of lightning in Rachel's head, and the hurt turned to white-hot anger. She said nothing. It wasn't worth the effort. It struck her that Brenna wasn't worth the effort.

"I'd like to stay, but I really must go. Send word if you decide to go tonight." Brenna picked up her reticule, gave Rachel a peck on the cheek, and hurried away.

They occasionally saw each other, but Brenna hadn't come to Emerson Manor in quite some time. Why did she come now? Rachel rose out of her seat in the carriage.

"Brenna?" Rachel called out as she stepped forward.

"I shouldn't be here," Brenna mumbled as she stopped drumming her fingers on the leather seat beside her and smacked her hand on the space.

Rachel stopped. No, Brenna shouldn't be here. Perhaps she shouldn't be here, either. Her best friend's betrayal was horrible, but Rachel had done worse. Much worse. Water over the dam, don't cry over spilled milk. Without any regret, Rachel moved past Brenna and left the carriage. A few seconds later, Brenna followed.

"Will you be leaving soon? I need to be back in Sommer-by-the-Sea," Brenna asked Mr. Wheeler.

"Yes, I'm going back now. I'll help you back in."

Brenna stared through her, turned on her heel, and boarded the carriage. Without a backward look, Brenna rode away.

"She has to live with the things she's done and come to terms with them," Rachel whispered, standing outside the manor entrance.

"Have you ever been inside?" Two women passed her on their way into the house. "I can't imagine living here. It looks like a palace from the outside, but the inside... this place is..."

Rachel looked at the four-story stone structure with spires and a witch's cap. Her lips turned into a smile. It did look like a castle. A few deep breaths, and she took a more critical look. Overall, the building and grounds appeared to have weathered the years well.

She walked into the entrance with its impressive variety of colored marble. The farther into the entranceway she walked, the more the years faded away until it was as if she had never been away. The doors from the entrance foyer into the house were wide open. She walked through the doorway and hurried to the center of the house.

Rachel stood in the Great Hall and looked at the massive forty-five-foot ceiling to the stained-glass skylight. Expansive overhanging balconies on the second and third floors narrowed the opening at the top. The architectural trick exaggerated the height of the room.

Oak railings rimmed the balconies. How often had a young Rachel peeked through the second-floor balusters to watch her parents' parties? And how often had her mother carried her to bed after she fell asleep on the balcony carpet?

Rachel twisted in all directions to get a better view. Above the first floor's oak wood panel, faded squares outlined where pictures and mirrors once hung on the Chinese red paper. The walls looked tired and old. Her stomach dropped—the furniture. Where did the large sideboards, the velvet sofa, and the central round table with Mother's prize Chinese jar go? Nothing remained except for the large grandfather clock and the flurry of activity around a small makeshift table.

Rachel came to Emerson Manor to surround herself with the comforts of home. That's what she told herself, but that wasn't the truth. Seeing the manor and experiencing nostalgia was nice, but that was not her mission. She reached for her locket, only to touch the empty spot at her throat. Lost years ago, an impulse demanded she find it. Ridiculous as it may be, the feeling persisted. The longer she put off the trip to Emerson Manor, the stronger the need grew until finding the locket became a compulsion, and her only thought. She'd torn the house apart years ago when she found it missing.

It's here. There was that whisper again. After all these years, could her golden heart be here?

The only way to quiet the voice was to look for the necklace. She'd start by searching each room, from the first floor to the fourth. Once she proved it wasn't here, she could leave and put this all to rest.

While the volunteers organized, Rachel stepped into the Green Salon to her right. Initially, the room was a formal ladies' reception area where her grandmother received visitors and served afternoon tea. When her parents owned the house, it was their private living room.

With the shades drawn, the room was dark. Light from the hall filtered in from behind her. The stale, musty odor of years of neglect surrounded her. She grew accustomed to the dark and realized this room, too, had no furniture. A search of the floor and an investigation of the alcoves on either side of the fireplace divulged nothing. The room was swept clean.

Back in the hall, she turned to the left and entered the billiard room, her grandfather and father's domain. They spent a great deal of time in here with their friends and their cigars. Gone was the oak and slate billiard table. The bar with the amber-colored bottles stood vacant. She searched the floor and shelves behind the bar, even her father's favorite secret compartment hidden in the wall but found nothing.

Rachel gripped the door handles to the adjoining library and hesitated. After a moment to collect her emotions, she stepped in. Her heart sank. Her father's grand desk, chair, and the leather-bound first editions that had filled the shelves were all gone.

After running her hands over all the shelves, she drew back. Rachel stabbed at her eyes to wipe away the tears. The hollow ache in her chest grew until it hurt to breathe.

"I waited too long," she whispered. Leaving the room behind, she went back to the Great Hall.

"Thank you all for coming today," Ina said from her perch at the back of the room. "The outpouring of help has been overwhelming. We've gone through the lists and given out assignments. We have more volunteers than we need. However, we're holding to our promise. You volunteered to get us ready, and to show our appreciation, the Emerson Foundation will give you two tickets to tonight's ball. Enjoy the house and grounds if you don't have an assignment today. Just a reminder, the other floors are closed to visitors. Also, make sure you're back here by three. The carriage will leave promptly. I'll give you your tickets to the ball then. Tickets will not be available in town.

"Now, if you're with the food this evening, please go into the dining room. You'll get your instructions there. Everyone else has their orders. Be here at three. I'm sure we can get everything done."

The hall emptied as the volunteers went to their assignments.

"You've done a wonderful job," Ina said to a man carrying a sack with tools. "I have two items on my list: the front light does not go on, and neither will some of the garden lights."

"That may be an easy issue to solve. I closed the gas line the last time I was here. I didn't want to leave the gas on without anyone living here."

Ina and the man headed to the front of the house.

Rachel entered the ballroom. Her thoughts drifted back to the days when the room was alive with people. The garden motif of the flowerlike crystal chandelier, sconces, and murals on the decorated plaster walls was still in place. She was seventeen.

"Father, we can't dance like this." Rachel stood defiantly in the ballroom with her parents. Her mother played the piano.

"Yes, I know. It's a waltz. Not for a father and daughter," her mother said. "But who else can teach you? Certainly not me."

"You mean holding you close and looking deeply into your eye," her father tried to hide his smile.

"Please!" Rachel rolled her eyes. "Fathers do not dance like that with their daughters, especially at their debut party. They do the quadrille, not the waltz.

"Besides, young ladies today do not have grand debut parties. I prefer a party on the beach." Rachel lifted her chin and met her mother's icy gaze. She wasn't going to let them see her withering inside. No, stick to your plan, *Brenna had told her.*

"Brenna's parents can make her a party on the beach. We thought a nice garden party with music. I want to be the first person with whom you waltz before you go off for your Season in London and waltz with some stranger at Almack's. You'll always be my princess."

She held him tight with no intention of letting him go. Ever.

Her parents were correct. The garden party was a success. Rachel had waltzed with her father and, later, caught a glimpse of her parents dancing in the darkened ballroom.

Her mother was unique, a blend of sophistication and whimsy. Her long silver hair was elegantly swept up and fastened away from her face, although long tendrils always seemed to get loose, much to her father's liking. Her sapphire blue eyes were expressive, and her smile was much like Father's mischievous, with hints of a playful sense of humor.

Her clothes were stylish but on the severe side, high neck bodices, long sleeves, and plain skirts. But it didn't matter what she wore. Mother always looked wonderful.

Rachel's memories were warm. Even the difficult ones had softened over the years. Was it fear of dredging up the past that made her fight returning to the manor? Time allowed her to believe the locket remained somewhere in the house, but standing here now, her mind was a combination of hope and fear. *Find it.* A small voice kept saying. *Find it.* Her dreams were bound up in that locket. He was bound up in the locket. Her time was running out. Midnight would come quickly enough.

Rachel left the ballroom and made her way to the grand stairs. Stanchions blocked the broad oak staircase, but that didn't stop her. She sidestepped the velvet ropes, climbed the stairs, and walked along the second-floor balcony that circled the Great Hall below. She stood with her back to the rail, the imposing doors to her parents' suite in front of her.

Large double doors to their apartment swung open into a small foyer. A private sitting room beyond separated her mother's boudoir on the right from her father's rooms on the left. At least the rooms were set up that way. Her mother never slept anywhere but with her father. Rachel walked through the empty space. The closet and drawers gaped open. Empty. Only thin layers of dust remained, along with a few stray buttons and memories.

She left their rooms and went down the hall. A thorough look at the four guest rooms, also void of furniture, yielded nothing. Her room was the last to search on this floor. Rachel braced herself outside her bedroom door. There was a very good reason to suspect her room would be as empty as the others. She took a deep breath for courage, pushed the door open, and stepped inside.

Soft floral paper covered the walls. Across from Rachel, large glass French doors led to a balcony overlooking the garden. The strained apprehension that dogged her all morning eased, but the push to move on continued.

Nothing remained in her dressing room. She opened her closet door and let out a small cry.

A series of pencil marks were etched alongside the door jamb. Each line included initials and a date. The Birthday Chart. Her fingers gently traced over the markings. Every birthday morning, one by one, each person stood against the wall to mark their height—Mother, Father, even Shotsy, their terrier. Her mother put her foot down when she wanted to measure Goldy, her fish.

Rachel returned to her bedroom and sat on the floor, her back against the wall. If the locket were anywhere in the house, it would be here. There were no drawers to look through, no pockets in clothes to rummage, no jewelry chest to inspect. Nothing.

She looked at the ceiling as if looking into the upper floors. The compulsion drove her, pushed her. No, the locket wasn't here, but there was still hope.

On her feet now, the servants' stairs were her goal. The hall clock struck the noon hour. That left twelve hours to explore the top two floors—*plenty of time.*

A mix of guest rooms and servant quarters occupied the third floor. Her investigation of these rooms revealed a few more buttons, some pennies, and a pencil—a bigger find in the servants' quarters: two metal bed frames stacked against the wall.

Satisfied there was nothing else to see, she climbed the narrow stairs to the fourth floor.

She stopped halfway up the stairs. Searching for the locket was ridiculous. Why had she thought the locket would be here? *Keep going.* Why was the constant voice urging her on when there was nothing to find? She waited for an answer. The voice was silent.

Shaking her head, she gave in to the request and continued to the fourth-floor landing. The thick layers of dust in the servants' quarters on this floor confirmed that no one used the rooms in decades.

Only her mother's tower room remained. Remote from the rest of the house, it was her mother's private perch. An urge pushed her toward the door. She reached out for the doorknob. It seemed to open by itself. Rachel stood in the doorway and imagined childhood squeals of laughter as she played some make-believe game with Brenna while her mother worked at her desk.

Light streamed into the whitewashed room from the oversize oval window. Wallpaper artfully hid the door to the right of the window that led outside to the narrow walkway around the witch's-cap roof. Few knew about the door. That made her smile.

She and Brenna had come up here to play and had watched through a slightly opened door as her mother opened the door and walked outside. Afterward, they would sneak into the room when her mother wasn't home and sit on the walkway. The fact that they could keep it from her mother was more reason to go out there.

Rachel stepped into the room, and her chest pounded. Her old, overstuffed chaise lounge chair, the one from her bedroom, was in the center of the room. Next to it was an open, partially filled trunk that begged to be inspected.

Chapter Three

Of all the furniture left in Emerson Manor, this chair was the most significant to Rachel. Lured farther into the room, she was tempted to sit in it one more time.

Her sense of loss was beyond tears. "Why is this chair the only piece of furniture in the entire house?" Her chest hurt like an old wound that ached on a rainy day.

Rachel stepped to the window and touched the fancy brass tack where her mother hung one of her favorite crystals to catch the light. *Activate it,* her mother told her. Father ignored the ritual. Rachel enjoyed the pretty prism of colors that danced on the wall when sunlight bathed the gem.

Tears welled up. She took a deep breath and turned toward the chair. She'd rest a few minutes, maybe look through the trunk so that coming here wasn't a complete waste of her time and energy.

She picked up a folio on the floor next to the trunk and sifted through it. Inside was a stack of clipped papers, random things: an old list of modistes in London, a receipt from the print shop, a paid bill from a caterer, a statement from the hospital, and another from the pharmacy. She put them aside and glanced in the trunk.

Copies of the *Sommer Sentinel*. Rachel knelt, reached in, and looked through the stack—all October editions dating as far back as 1789.

She sat back on her heels. Did she want to go through these? It pained her when she packed this trunk. How much better would it be now?

The box of October newspapers had been her idea of a keepsake to be opened in the future. They should have tossed out the newspapers with the furniture. Why had anyone kept them? Her joyless laugh echoed in the room. She quieted as she glanced around the room. Someone wanted her to find them.

Rachel picked up a newspaper from the top of the stack. October 1804. She opened the scandal sheet. Below the fold, a hand-drawn picture of Emerson Manor's front door, decorated for autumn.

"Here, Rachel, have some of your mother's special brew. She promised a special costume for dinner. Any idea what it is?" her father asked.

"No, she's been very mysterious."

Dressed in formal dinner clothes, Father poured the ruby-red drink and plopped an ice cube into the glass. Mrs. Reid, wearing a beautifully jeweled and feathered half mask, placed the soup tureen by Mother's plate. Everyone at Emerson Manor dressed for All Hallows Eve.

"Mrs. Reid, you look lovely this evening." Her father smirked over his drink.

"Thank you, Your Grace," she said, then left.

"Mrs. Reid has been preening with the mask all afternoon. Where did you find it?"

"In London. I knew the feathers would catch her attention." He opened the tureen and swished through the soup. "No eyeballs this year."

Father sat in his chair and swallowed his drink as Mother quietly entered the room dressed all in black. I never thought someone's eyes could bulge so dramatically until I looked at Father. He spit his drink across the table in a fine spray.

The sight of her mother, who wore her blouses buttoned to her nose and skirts down to her ankles in a snug-fitting, hide-almost-nothing-from-sight dress, was compelling. She looked… wonderful.

After a quiet moment, the three of them burst out laughing.

"You are worth waiting for, Edythe." The tone of her father's voice sounded soft and seductive. Her parents were private people, not prone to public displays of affection, but much like they forgot the servants were in the room, they seemed to have forgotten she dined with them that night.

When Rachel realized that her father was… aroused in that way, she wanted to hide. Brenna told her all about 'that.' Her parents. Together. Like that. She erased the picture from her head.

Father rose and gave Mother her drink, then helped her to her chair. He took off his jacket and draped it on her shoulders. Bending beside her, he whispered in her ear. Her mother's flush started at her throat and raced up her face, which held an innocent smile. God's teeth, she wanted to hear what Father had said. He had to have said something swoon-worthy because Mother playfully took his face in her hands and kissed his lips.

Rachel coughed. Loud. Her father raised an eyebrow at her, a broad smile. He kissed her mother's forehead and returned to his chair. Although aware her parents loved each other, this was the first time she was privy to their emotions. The dress had little to do with it, although Mother looked beautiful. To be cherished so deeply by another must be marvelous indeed. The yearning for such a love swelled within her heart, a love that held the promise of eternal joy, a love that would endure forever.

After Mother's grand entrance, dinner moved on as usual. Mrs. Reid's mask didn't resurface until later in the evening when the guests began to arrive.

Mother's black dress was for Father only. She changed into a more respectable witch costume. Mother always wore a witch costume. It was her signature statement for the ball. Each year she found something more fantastic than the year before.

Father usually wore his dinner clothes, but he was a dashing sheik this year.

Rachel smiled at the newspaper picture. She had worn a long slender black dress. Mrs. Reid helped paint a white streak down the middle of her long black hair.

"Rachel, come here," her mother called from the ballroom door.

Rachel dragged herself away from her friends. She made her way through the crush of people—footmen carrying drinks and serving hors d'oeuvres.

Finally, Rachel approached her mother through the crowd. Her step faltered. Pryce stood with his parents. Dressed in evening attire, Pryce didn't need a costume to attract attention. The girls in the room gave him a hungry stare.

"There you are. Rachel, may I introduce you to Lord Somerset, the son of the Duke and Duchess of Ashworth?"

"Lord Somerset, it is a pleasure to make your acquaintance." Rachel couldn't help but give him a broad smile.

"My lady, I assure you that the pleasure is entirely mine." His eyes twinkled and his smile… It was charming.

"Somerset was just telling me that he's returning to my old school, Oxford University, in January." Father had a particular softness for anyone who attended Oxford. "Why don't you introduce him to your friends?"

She and Pryce walked through the room.

"Pryce, what a delightful surprise to see you here," Brenna purred, intertwining her arm with his. Rachel simmered with frustration. Did Brenna think for a minute that she could assert herself? Of course, she did.

Pryce gently removed Brenna's hand from his and grabbed two glasses of punch from the footman as he went by. He handed one to her and the other to Rachel.

"Miss Brenna, if you'll excuse us. Lady Rachel and I have some things to discuss." He turned to Rachel. "It's too loud in here. Is there someplace we can go?"

It was Brenna's turn to fume, but her scathing glare missed its mark. Pryce had outwitted her.

"Discuss?" Rachel said over the music. Her insides tingled, and her heart fluttered whenever he looked at her.

"That girl corners—"

"Come with me. I know a place where we can talk without being interrupted." Rachel downed her drink in two gulps, put her empty glass on a table, and led the way out the French doors to the garden. The music faded the farther they moved away from the house. It turned into a soft buzz by the time they reached the far edge of the garden and turned the corner.

"That's better," Pryce said. He looked around. "Where are we?"

"In the far corner of the estate, near the cemetery. I found this place when I was ten. My parents made me stay in my room for something I'd done. I searched for the most remote part of the grounds where no one would find me. The fact that it's next to the cemetery seemed perfect at the time, if a bit dramatic. Over the years, the tree became my confidant." She was blabbering. Nervous? Would he think her crazy?

He walked around the large tree and tested a low-hanging branch. "That girl, Brenna, corners me whenever she sees me. I feel like I'm a prize piece of meat she can't wait to devour." He turned to Rachel, a broad smile on his face. "I feel better already."

There was no mocking expression on his face or tone in his voice. Rachel was interested in him even more.

"I came here to meet you under better circumstances." He faced her squarely. His voice rang with sincerity. "I'm sorry about the other day in town. The road was clear one minute, and the next, you were in front of me. You stood in the road like a startled hind. I couldn't stop the carriage fast enough."

"It must be our destiny," she said, a teasing tone in her voice. "I had looked before I crossed. I'm always careful, especially at The Bend."

"The Bend?" His lips pursed as he bit the side of his mouth. She suspected it was to stifle a laugh.

"It's not funny. You can't see around the curve, and you gather speed because of the sudden dip in the road. Everyone in town knows about it."

He ran his hand through his hair. "I guess I do, too. Now."

"Anyway, I looked, and the street was empty. Suddenly, you were there."

She stared into his eyes. Even in the dim light, she noticed they had changed from hazel to a heart-stopping shade of blue. She could get lost in those eyes. They were soft, intelligent, and proud. What shade would his eyes be if he looked at her the same way her father looked at her mother at dinner? The idea made her breathless.

"Skunk," he said, looking at her costume.

"In tribute to our first encounter." Then, more solemnly, she added, "I hoped you would be here tonight."

"Even skunks couldn't keep me away." He took her hand. They walked back to the garden, where they sat and talked about everything from their childhoods to their near-miss accident.

The music, which was tolerable in the garden, stopped. A clock chimed from somewhere in the house. Rachel stood up.

"Cinderella?" he asked.

Rachel laughed. "No. It's the witching hour. Mother, as the witch of the evening, overdramatizes the hour. According to her, magic is at its strongest at midnight. We should get back. We don't want to miss the fireworks. Those are at midnight, too."

"I want to see you again," Pryce said with a bit of urgency. "Tomorrow."

"At the oak tree. We can meet there whenever you like." Rachel smiled.

"How will I know you'll be there?" he teased.

"I'll leave you a note in the afternoon." Her arm linked in his, *they strolled into the ballroom.*

Their connection was immediate, and she knew they would always be for each other. There would never be anyone else.

Now, Rachel tried to look into the garden through the oval window but couldn't see through the dirt and grime. Mrs. Reid would never tolerate this. She rubbed the window to clean a spot for a better view, but the dirt must've been on the outside.

She jockeyed around the window until she found a clearer spot and could see the end of the formal garden at the back of the house. The overgrown hedgerow hid any view of the oak tree. The gardener had left his tools there, waiting.

Her forehead on the cold glass cooled her long-forgotten emotions that bubbled to the surface. Sentiments never spoken were on her lips. She had tried to forget Pryce, but he had been with her always.

Rachel searched the old knothole. Her heart sank to her toes and back to her chest. Meet me tonight. P.

It was the end of the summer, the night before Pryce returned to Oxford. She fidgeted all through a torturous dinner. Would dinner never end? Finally able to slip away, she flew across the garden. Out of breath, her smile broadened when she turned the corner. Pryce stood by the tree.

"Is everything all right? I thought you were going to stay home with your parents."

He took her in his arms. "I love you. From the very first moment, I saw you. I was so struck by the feeling that I nearly ran you over. We belong together."

He took her by her shoulders and held her at arm's length. "You know that, don't you?"

Rachel stared into his brilliant, intelligent eyes, and her pulse raced. Unable to find her voice, she could only nod a response. Was this just a summer flirtation? Brenna had spent the past few days preparing her for Pryce to cast her aside. Would he go back to Oxford and forget all about Sommer-by-the-Sea—all about her?

He pulled her close and tucked her head under his chin. *"I love you,"* he whispered into her hair.

"I love you, too." The words fell easily from her lips. She had been saying them to herself for days.

He put something in her hand. Startled, she looked in her palm. It was a locket.

"Forever, Rachel." With shaking hands, he put the locket around her neck as she stared at him, speechless and jubilant—her Pryce.

"There," he said when he finished. His chest thrust out, and his shoulders went back. Rachel stretched on her tippy toes, threw her arms around his neck, and smiled when she looked into his eyes. They changed to that heart-stopping blue when they were filled with love.

"I'll never take it off," she murmured against his lips and kissed him, then turned to leave.

"Don't go back yet. Stay with me a little longer." He hadn't let go of her hand.

Her heart pounded.

They sat by the tree and watched the stars, his arm around her shoulder.

"That's Orion. Can you see the three stars that make up the belt?" He pointed somewhere in the sky, but she wasn't looking. His lips held her attention.

He looked at her and stopped talking. He had happily-ever-after written all over his face. His lips captured hers. Gentle at first, his kiss became more urgent.

She molded into his arms and never wanted him to let go. He hesitated a heartbeat, then raised his lips from hers. He lifted her and carried her through the garden to the patio door.

Rachel stood there, her body in revolt. She wanted more. She wanted Pryce.

"I don't love you like that." His expression was severe.

She sucked in a quick breath, tears welling in her eyes.

"I love you more. I want it to be right." His forehead rested against hers. "I cherish you deeply. My feelings for you are deep and sincere."

He kissed her and nudged her to the door.

She watched him cross the garden, waved when he reached the dogleg and disappeared.

"Was that Pryce?" her mother asked as Rachel entered the living room.

Unable to get any words out, she nodded.

Her mother lowered the book she was reading. "Is everything all right?" Concern filled her mother's voice.

"Yes," she whispered and sat next to her mother. "I'll miss him."

"Yes, I know you will." Her mother glanced at her neck and smiled. "Did he give you the locket?"

She'd forgotten all about the locket. "Yes." Her hand touched the small heart.

Mother kissed her forehead. "He'll be home soon."

Rachel didn't want him home soon. That wasn't fair, but her heart didn't want fair. Her heart wanted Pryce. She said good night to her mother, rushed into her room, and removed the necklace.

Delicate gold filigree and small diamonds decorated the outside. Carefully she opened it to look inside.

My heart is yours—Forever.

She held his heart close to hers.

Chapter Four

Rachel moved away from the window and stood behind the chaise lounge, her hand resting on the blanket draped on the back of the chair. Forever. Nothing was forever. Not friends, not... She sat in the chair and took the stack of papers from the trunk.

And the locket. How could the locket be lost? She went over the day a hundred, a thousand times.

"Are you sure you had it here?" Her mother looked through Rachel's jewelry box. When she didn't find the locket, she moved on to her nightstand drawer.

"Of course, I'm sure. I never take it off." Rachel pulled the linen off the bed and left it in a heap on the floor. Mrs. Reid methodically went through each fold before tossing it into the hall.

"When did you notice it missing?"

"I told you," she barked at her mother. "I stood at the sink washing my face. I didn't have my locket on."

"I'm sure Pryce will replace the locket if you tell him what happened."

"No. I can't tell him." She wheeled around. Her stomach clenched tight. She grabbed her mother's hands. "Promise me you won't say a word about this to him."

"Of course, I won't." Her mother's slow, uneven tone made her stop and drop her hands.

"I could replace it, have it engraved? No one would know."

Her mother's concern was written on her face.

"No. It has to be the one Pryce gave me. Not a replacement from you or him." The duchess opened her arms. Rachel stepped into her embrace and sobbed. "Don't you understand?"

"Shush. Everyone is looking for it. We'll find it. It couldn't vanish." Her mother moved the hair out of her eyes. "Tell me about your visit with Brenna. How late did she stay last night? I didn't see her leave."

"Not too late. About eight. We were trying on clothes to decide what to wear to Mrs. Bainbridge's luncheon next week."

The empty, sinking feeling flashed through her; her loss was as deep now as when she'd realized the locket was gone. She loosened her death grip on the blanket crumpled in her fist. All that was left of his love was the locket. She had to find it.

"You've come this far," she told herself. "See it through. Go through the trunk. Finish the task. Don't give up now. Just because no one could find the locket then doesn't mean searching for it now is useless."

She warred with herself. "Listen to me. There. Is. No. Place. Else. To. Search." What perverse need drove her? There wasn't any way the locket was in the trunk. If she gave up now, she'd stop driving herself crazy, but the image of the locket swirled in her head.

The musty room closed in around her. Some invisible force sucked all the air out. She tugged at the neck of her dress without relief. She needed fresh air. Pulling on the small door to the upper walk was useless; it wouldn't budge. She rushed out of the room with the newspapers in her hand.

The image of the locket faded when she reached the second floor. She calmly came down the stairs on steadier legs. Cool air, with a hint of lemon, cleared her mind by the time she reached the first floor.

"Put this under that bottle. I don't want a pool of oil on the stairs," Ina said to Nora. At least that was the name on the tag she wore on her Sommer-by-the-Sea Housekeepers apron.

Nora took a scrap of newspaper and put it under the bottle as Ina asked.

"Well done. Mrs. Reid always used lemon oil," Rachel said, stepping past them.

"Yes, the lemon oil is best," Ina said as Nora tested a spot on the railing.

"That's better. I knew the mahogany would shine. Stop at the second-floor landing. We don't need the rest done for tonight." Ina hurried into the dining room.

Rachel left Nora and made her way onto the veranda.

"Will we have lights tonight?" Ina asked as she left the dining room doors with the man, who still carried a sack of tools, and went down the veranda steps. He must have finished working on the gaslights in front.

"There are several gaslights out here that still need to be fixed. I'll have them all working before three, as you asked."

"This is coming along nicely. Let me know when you're finished with your work." Ina started toward the house.

"Is there anything you'd like me to do?" Rachel asked.

The woman waved. Rachel took that as a no. Ina had already disappeared into the house.

Rachel took a deep breath of the cool air. Overhead, the distinctive sound of honking geese drew her attention as they flew in a chevron pattern. She watched them fly until they were out of sight, then stepped into the garden.

Fallen leaves tumbled across the lawn. The bushes were trimmed, and the flower beds along the perimeter of the path were prepared for the winter. Close to the grove of maple and copper beech trees were gardening tools that looked out of place. The last time the gardener brought those tools into the garden, he removed large dead trees. From her vantage point, the maples and beeches looked healthy. Her oak tree was the only other large tree in that area.

They wouldn't take the oak tree down, would they?

Rachel hurried to the end of the garden and navigated past the gardening tools. At the turn where the garden doglegged to the right, she suddenly stopped. This area of the property, hidden from the manor, hadn't been maintained as well as the rest of the garden. Bushes and trees had gone wild and needed trimming. That would have to wait until the spring. Leaves covered the lawn, but that didn't matter. In the distance, the massive oak kept watch over the garden and the cemetery.

She plowed through the piles of neglected leaves until she stood at the base of the tree. She ran her hand over the rough bark, her touch reconnecting with her old friend.

The tree and Rachel had a long history together. This was her go-to place when she wanted to be alone and work things out. The silent sentinel heard it all and didn't judge. As a child, she left notes in an old knothole. When she grew older, she left messages for Pryce—their place. Silly, but the oak tree became special to them both.

"I should have brought something that says I was here." For a frantic minute, she searched the ground but found nothing meaningful, and suddenly that was very important.

She patted her clothes and pulled the note out of her pocket. *Meet me tonight. R.*

"Of course." The note was perfect. It belonged in the tree. She tucked it into their special place.

How many times did I stand here arguing with myself? I should have put this note here long ago when there was a chance that Pryce would read it.

Rachel tenderly touched the tree and then stepped back. Did the day look brighter? No, but the unfinished task had weighed heavily on her mind. Now completed, there was relief and even some satisfaction.

The gnarled roots still provided a comfortable seat. Rachel sat with the papers tucked in her lap, her arms around her knees, and savored being under the tree once again.

She uncurled and opened the 1805 newspaper and stared at the hand-drawn picture of the All Hallows Eve revelers. Everyone was looking up. The drawing was done with the artist looking down from the second-floor balcony into the Great Hall. One by one, she identified everyone and stopped when Pryce came into view with his arm around her shoulder.

"Should I wear the red shoes or the black ones?" Rachel asked Brenna as they dressed for the ball.

"Why are you so picky? You never cared before." Brenna looked at Rachel's reflection in the large mirror as they prepared for the ball.

"I've always been picky. You just haven't noticed." She chose the black shoes.

"You don't know if he's even coming. I'm sure there are all sorts of parties at Oxford that are more interesting than this ball." Brenna tried on Rachel's chandelier earrings. She admired them from every angle, put the earrings down, and tried on the next pair.

"Come on. Are you ready? Mother prefers I help her greet people at the door." Her shoes on, Rachel stuck her head next to Brenna's to get a last look before they went downstairs. "I'll leave without you."

Brenna grabbed her arm and swung her around.

"What?" Rachel was in no mood for drama or games.

"Listen, this relationship you think you have with Pryce will not come to anything. I know the others have told you how perfect you are for each other but be realistic. There's no such thing as happily-ever-after. Don't fill your head with such nonsense. You'll only come away disappointed. He's a gorgeous man at the university. Yes, it's nice he

comes home and sees you, but I don't want you to be devastated when he outgrows you and moves on to his next interest."

Not my... Moves on? Pryce? Rachel smiled at her friend. "That's not going to happen. You'll see."

Brenna dropped her hand and sighed. "Don't say I didn't warn you."

"Are you going to wear those?" Rachel looked at the earrings her father had bought her from India a few months ago.

"You don't mind, do you? You're not wearing them, and I do love them." Brenna shook her head and made the tiny bells tinkle.

"No, that's fine. Just put the earrings back before you leave."

"Of course," Brenna said as they walked out the door.

At the top of the staircase, Rachel stopped and searched the crowd for Pryce. He stood at the bottom of the steps smiling at her.

She rushed down the stairs, leaving Brenna to trail behind. In a gallant gesture, he kissed her hand. The scent of his cologne...

She lowered her hands, and the newspaper wrinkled in her lap. A deep breath conjured up the citrus and woodsy fragrance of Pryce's cologne. Her lips tingled from the memory of his kiss.

They were rarely apart after that visit. Even though Oxford was a full day's ride away, Pryce came home most weekends, sometimes during the week. She continued at Mrs. Bainbridge's Seminary.

Rachel folded the newspaper, put it aside, and looked at the next one. October 1806. Nothing significant on the front. She turned the pages. This was her favorite edition. It was worn from being read over and over. The Society page had an interview with her mother about the masquerade ball. Lower down was an article about Brenna and Huntley Andrews, her Cambridge University sweetheart, and their September wedding.

"Rachel." Brenna stuck her head in the room where the bridesmaids were getting ready. Sarah Andrews, Huntley's sister, attended Brenna. They were both in the room next to Rachel.

"Sarah is wonderful," Brenna whispered, "but has no idea what needs to be done. Can you check on the kitchen? Huntley loves hot chocolate with cinnamon, and I want to ensure the drink is prepared perfectly. Oh, and can you make sure Father Henderson has the names correct?" Brenna began to withdraw when she again put her head through the door. "Mother has hired a harpist and violinist." Brenna reached into her bodice and drew out a piece of paper. "I do not trust Mother's choice in music. Please give this to them."

"Of course." There was plenty of time for her to finish dressing. Rachel turned to leave.

"I'll be right there," Brenna shouted over her shoulder.

"Our friends—"

"Speaking about our friends," Brenna interrupted Rachel, "can you see to them? You know, make sure they have whatever they need. Mother will be occupied with our family while Mother Andrews and I see to that side of the family. Now I must go." Brenna closed the door before Rachel responded.

Hours later, after the ceremony and morning meal were over, she finally sat next to Pryce.

"Are you finished? Or has the bride more for you to do?" He handed her a glass of champagne. "What was all the commotion between the happy couple?"

"Huntley wanted to leave."

"Ah, but Brenna wanted to stay."

Rachel glanced at the buffet table. Most of the food had been eaten. Even the pot of hot chocolate at the end of the table was empty. The only thing left was for Brenna and Huntley to cut the wedding cake.

"It's not that bad. Brenna's excited and wants everything to be right. Every girl wants her day to be perfect." Drained from running around, Rachel sipped her drink and looked at the barely touched eggs and bacon on her plate.

"*I don't think your friends are taking it so casually.*" Pryce nodded across the room.

"*You and Brenna have been friends all your life. She has you running all over instead of enjoying your meal, or your friends, or dancing with me.*" He waved to get the footman's attention.

The footman set a plate covered with a cloche in front of her.

"*What's this?*"

"*I asked Mrs. Haskell for a meal for you.*"

Rachel whipped around and stared at him. "*You know the Hutchington's cook?*"

Pryce turned her back toward the table, shook out the folded serviette, and placed it on her lap. "*I do now. I went inside and told her how hard you worked and how hungry you were. She told me, 'Anything for Lady Rachel.'*" The footman removed the cloche and revealed a warm bilberry scone, eggs, and fresh bacon.

"*Have I told you lately, my lord, that I love you?*" She made herself comfortable, buttered her scone, and bit into it. He dabbed her chin with his serviette to catch a rivulet of butter.

"*Thank you,*" she mumbled, her mouth full. Pryce relaxed and smiled. Her heart pounded as she lifted her champagne.

"*You're welcome. I am here only to serve you.*" He bobbed his head in a slight bow. "*And you tell me you love me all the time. In the way you look at me, listen to my plans...*" he leaned close and whispered in her ear, "*and the way you kiss me.*"

Her champagne glass froze in midair. She was willing not to stay for the rest of the meal and sneak away with him now.

"*May I have everyone's attention, please?*" One of Brenna's friends, Carnaby, the Earl of Wentworth, the son of the Marquess of Lofton, stood in the middle of the room.

"*To the bride and groom.*" He lifted his glass. "*May she be strong enough to endure his fits of temper and proclivity for...*" There was a long pause. "*I'll leave that to your imagination. Andrew, you have accumulated a king's ransom. Let's hope you can hold on to it.*"

Andrew's face burned red with anger as he pulled his bride from the feast. The earl and his countess said their goodbyes as quickly as possible. The bride and groom were gone before Rachel could say anything to Brenna.

No one understood her relationship with Brenna. Rachel shook her head. On occasion, neither did she. Rachel lowered the newspaper. Why did Brenna come to Emerson Manor today? There were times when Brenna was all like a sister, an absolute best friend, but now she couldn't get far enough away from her.

Rachel folded the newspaper and reached for the next, October 1808. It was open to the Society page. "Earl Somerset Christens Boat at Emerson Boathouse and Wins Prize." Rachel could recite this article word for word.

"You coming? We'll leave without you." Rachel's mother shouted from downstairs.

Rachel grabbed her reticule, hurried out of her room, and ran down the stairs. "What's the hurry? We have a half hour before we have to be there." She paused in front of the Great Hall mirror for a final check of her new blue-and-white-striped cotton summer dress.

"You look fine, dear. Your father's waiting for us outside." Her mother slipped her arm around her as they left the house, almost pushing her out the door.

"Ah, my girls." Father rubbed his hands together and practically danced from one foot to the other. She was sure he would fly off if her mother hadn't threaded her arm through his.

"No holding my nose today." His eyes twinkled as he covered Mother's hand with his.

"I was thinking the same thing," Rachel said. "That was so long ago."

"Not to me," her father said in a low whisper.

They came down the trail and around to the front of the boathouse. Pryce worked all summer and fall repairing the old sailboat. Now he stood in the center of a crowd of friends and family.

The boat was turned around with its stern facing the crowd. A wrapped bottle stood next to it. A white canvas covered the transom. Their friends had been taking bets on what he would name the boat. Nobody knew, not even her.

Pryce broke away from the crowd and came toward them. He held her with his eyes. God's teeth, she would love him forever.

"Glad you could make it." He smirked.

"From the look on your face, I'd say it was worth waiting for." She kissed his nose. "Okay, I can't wait. What did you name her?"

It was her turn to bounce from foot to foot. The four of them walked to the pier.

"Come on, Pryce. There's a lot of money riding on what you named her," one of their friends shouted. Everyone laughed.

He grabbed Rachel's hand and walked to the dock. Everyone moved in to hear and see the big reveal.

"I love you, Rachel," he said, loud enough for everyone to hear.

"I know," she whispered. "Pryce, what are you doing? Not here."

He pulled off the canvas to a thunder of gasps. Rachel turned and could only stare at the name painted on the bow.

Marry Me.

She looked back at him. He knelt in front of her with something sparkling in his hand.

The water gently lapping against the dock, and the soft murmur of the fall wind in the trees, were the only sounds, except for her heart. Surely, everyone could hear it hammering against her chest.

She bent down and pulled him up.

"I adore you," he said for her ears only.

"As I do you. Forever," Rachel said, then threw her arms around him.

Their family and friends erupted with cheers. Smiles spread quickly, and laughter filled the air as family and friends embraced Pryce and Rachel.

"Enough, you two." Brenna handed Pryce the covered bottle. "You're launching more than a boat, so be careful."

Pryce gave the bottle to her. "Aim for the metal edge."

One swing and foam and champagne exploded everywhere.

"Congratulations." Her father held her tight and looked over at Pryce. "This public proposal is… well, it's not natural. But for Rachel, I will do anything."

"As will I, Your Grace," Pryce responded to her father, but his eyes never left Rachel.

"I know you will," her father affirmed.

Pryce's parents were next. "We couldn't be happier."

But she didn't see them, her family, or their friends. Only Pryce.

After the toasts and handshakes, her father ushered them onto the boat.

"You both get in the boat. I'll be your crew."

Pryce raised the jib, luffing in the wind as her father skillfully guided the boat to the end of the dock. Pryce pushed the tiller windward and set the jib to catch the wind and get enough speed to clear the dock. The bow of the boat came parallel to the end of the pier, pointed into the channel. He raised the main sail and picked up speed.

"Enjoy your sail," her father called. "Be back in time for your mother's ball."

Everyone waved as Pryce sailed the boat out into the bay.

They anchored the boat by the small island a few miles from the town docks. The barren island was nothing more than a beach and a few trees.

Pryce sat on the boat, his back against the gunwale. She cuddled close, tucked under his arm, and stared at the ring on her finger.

"You should have seen your face." He chuckled, low and wicked. She whirled to face him. His eyes pinned her like a fly in amber.

"What did I look like?" She blew out her breath and licked her lips.

"Shocked and happy. I don't think I've ever seen you so… happy." He pulled her onto his lap. "I love you. I knew it the first time I saw you."

"Lying on the road? That's a novel way to meet someone."

He held her tight. Two heartbeats passed before he whispered, "I'll love you forever." His voice deepened as the glint in his eyes darkened. He kissed the pulsing hollow at the base of her throat.

His lips covered hers like a hot brand. His hands slid down her legs. His kiss never stopped. Lost in his love, she encouraged him to go on. His hand stroked her calf and her thigh.

Rachel imagined every inch of her body craving his touch.

He pulled away from her, seeking encouragement and agreement to go on.

She surrendered to her happy ever after.

He stood and lifted her into his arms. They spent the rest of the day in the cabin as the boat bobbed in the water.

Now, the folded paper was lying in her lap. The vision faded as Rachel leaned against the oak tree, but the memory… lingered, and she had no intention of giving it up quickly.

Chapter Five

Lights flickered in the distance. The workman must have left the gaslights on. An onshore breeze picked up, sending leaves into small whirls. Clouds gathered in the east. It would be a pity if it rained after everyone's hard work.

One more unread newspaper remained, and she wasn't eager to read it. Rachel rose, picked up the papers, and returned to the manor.

She took the long way back, past the stables and the barn, then alongside the manor to the front entrance. A plume of dust traveled down the drive as the back of the carriage wound its way toward Manor Road. She had lost track of time.

The clouds hadn't gotten any more ominous. Rachel hurried to the entrance, intent on returning the newspapers to the trunk. With any luck, the rain might hold off until she got away.

A black-and-orange wreath hung on the manor door. Glittery leaves hung in the corners of the entryway.

The door squeaked open, making Rachel chuckle, remembering how Mrs. Reid kept the hinges oiled until August. She resumed oiling them on November 1. During the ball, her mother insisted that the door be slowly opened so everyone could hear the eerie noise.

Inside, the large round table was back in the center of the Great Hall, covered with a black lace cloth. In the center of the table, oversized long-stem black roses were in the cut glass urn with its four feet. A large card on a small easel said Welcome to the Lady Emerson's Masquerade Ball.

She peeked into the ballroom. Black drapes hung beside the floor-to-ceiling doors that led to the veranda. Full-size silhouettes peered into the room from every glass door. The silky gauze that hung from the ceiling was sprinkled with glitter that would glisten in the candlelight.

The theme carried into the dining room. Tables were set with black linens and white plates. The centerpiece on each table was a tall white vase with a candle inside waiting to be lit.

Buffet stations lined the walls. The serving dishes waiting to be filled. A bar ran across the entire back wall. Everything was ready.

Rachel went to the staircase—another masquerade ball. Her mother began planning the next one the day after the event. Mother would approve of the dramatic decor. Rachel wasn't sure who enjoyed the event more, her mother or the community.

Years ago, Rachel began saving the October newspapers to remember each party. She used to enjoy reading them. They became treasured keepsakes. Now, what sense did it make? Nothing could be changed, and the outcome—well, she knew all too well the outcome.

Why had she put herself through this? The love and disappointment hurt as much now as before. It was time to put the newspapers away and leave them to the past where they belonged. Then, she would be on her way.

Easing past the stanchion guarding the stairs, she climbed to the second floor. A scrap of oily newspaper sat abandoned on the landing. It was from last Sunday's edition of the *Sommer Sentinel.* It must have been the paper Nora used under the bottle of lemon oil. Rachel picked it up.

There was a teaser about the new representative to the House of Commons, Evan Washburn, but the headline concentrated on the upcoming masquerade ball. It listed the members of the committee, along with sponsors for the event. Ah, now she understood why Brenna came to the manor. She was the committee chair. Rachel read the list of supporters, and her heart did a small flip. Somerset Brokerage headed the sponsor list, but the gossip item in the sidebar made her tremble.

Pryce Drake, the Earl of Somerset Returns Home. Known for his philanthropy over the years, the retired financial expert behind the London investment group Somerset Brokerage—

Rachel flipped the page over for the rest of the article. The information covered something about the local Garden Club but nothing about Pryce.

Her mother's masquerade ball. He never missed it. Was that the real reason she waited until today to come back? No, she didn't need to be here to think about him. Pryce was part of her daily routine.

She spent her day reliving things they did together, his touch, his kiss, and even his love. He had been so real.

Maybe if she stayed… Her lower lip trembled as the notion took root. See Pryce one more time. No, no, impossible. Face him now and see the hate in his eyes. That would be too much to bear.

Letting things be was the only answer. Enjoy the memories. *There's nothing to be gained from what could have been.* Yes, better to let things be after all this time. Standing in the middle of the second-floor landing with the last newspaper in Rachel's hand, she wanted to cry, but the tears wouldn't come.

She sat on the top step and opened the newspaper. October 1810.

Everything was arranged. Pryce started at a new company in London the previous May, and they set off on a new adventure. For six months, they traveled between London and Sommer-by-the-Sea.

Thumbing through the paper, she read the wedding announcement her mother had prepared.

They were both home for the October event, planning their Christmas wedding. Addressed invitations sat bundled in the library, ready to be mailed the following day, the same day Pryce was to return to London.

"If I knew you were dressing as Cleopatra, I would have come as Mark Antony, my queen." Pryce dipped an elegant bow, then kissed her on her nose. "Where's your mother? I expected to see her at the door. What type of witch is she this year?"

In a dashing pirate costume, the top button of his shirt open, Pryce searched the decorated ballroom for Lady Emerson. "I wanted to tell her about the arrangements with the musicians for our wedding and say goodbye. I have to leave early in the morning and won't have time to see you or your family before I go."

Rachel didn't answer. She had been dealing with so much the past two weeks.

"You're going to get a permanent wrinkle on your forehead if you don't stop frowning." He kissed her worry spot.

"Let's go outside. We need to talk," Rachel said, her throat tight and her voice high-pitched. For days she practiced this speech and chose her words carefully. Now that the time had come to talk, the words were all wrong. She licked her parched lips. The two glasses of liquid courage she'd had earlier weren't helping. And the possibility of a last-minute reprieve she had hoped for had vanished ninety minutes ago. She wanted to hide somewhere and cry.

He leaned against the veranda's wide stone railing, his arms comfortably folded while she paced in front of him.

"What's this about? The flowers? The caterer?" His voice—soft,

male, and mellow—had her thinking of other things. Things that were no longer within her right to dream about.

"No." If only it were that simple. She stood not close enough for him to hold her. That would be a disaster.

"Over the last few months, Mother hasn't been well." Rachel stepped back, her eyes anywhere but on him. Stop now. There's still time. Tell him the truth—*one deep, steadying breath. The rehearsed words flew out of her head. For a moment, she faltered and thought she couldn't go through with it. The truth was on her lips.* Do what's best for him. For Pryce, do you hear?

"We noticed it in May and thought it was overwork and not enough sleep. It progressively got worse."

Coward. *Rachel watched him out of the corner of her eye. He dropped his arms and straightened from his slouch.*

"Is your mother all right? Should we call someone? I'll call Dr. Manning." Rachel loved him more for his genuine concern.

"We've been to several doctors, including Dr. Manning. Each one gave us the same prognosis. Father and I were more than surprised. The decline will be rapid at first, but she'll linger for some time. They told us there is little hope for recovery but added that new protocols emerge every day." Her voice trailed off. Her eyes closed. The words made everything real.

"I can't leave her now. With my father's heavy business schedule, there's no one but me. Once her condition stabilizes, we can see about continuing our plans." How sterile and unemotional that sounded.

"I'll stay in Sommer-by-the-Sea. There's no need to change our plans." It was an order. He sounded like he was negotiating a business deal, not their lives. No, that wasn't fair. He was fighting for them, something she'd given up after a disappointing conversation when reality hit her. The war was lost. There was no need for her to keep fighting. Now he had to understand. He had to go on.

"This is going to be a long, drawn-out process. Right now, I have to take care of Mother without any distractions." She was adamant, but the hurt in his eyes was a dagger in her heart.

"As soon as Mother's stable. It's only a delay," she lied.

She watched emotions cross his face and knew the moment he understood her meaning. She shriveled at his expression. They both were going to lose everything, and there was nothing for her to do but watch.

He gave her a curt nod. His face told her nothing. "Let's get back inside."

"I was afraid… I didn't know if you'd want to…" God's teeth, this was going all wrong. There was no way to take back the words or tell him the whole truth. If he knew, he'd never leave her.

He pulled her into his arms and held her close. "It's October 30th. I never miss an Edythe Emerson Masquerade Ball."

Every minute he held her, she died a little more. She wouldn't leave his embrace until she memorized every nuance. It had to last her a long time. There would be no happy ever after.

"No, you don't, and I wouldn't want you to start now." She forced a cheery smile.

"Truce?" he asked.

"Truce." He put his arm around her waist and brought her inside.

They smiled at the toasts offered for their marriage. They danced and forgot anyone else was in the room. They ate with their friends and told terrible jokes. The mayor's wife, dressed as Joan of Arc, won the costume award. Rachel's parents won the waltz contest.

Rachel lost everything.

At the end of the evening, when everyone was gone, they walked to the oak tree. Pryce looked in the knothole.

"No note."

"No, I have you here with me," she said, squeezing him.

Silence.

"I'm not sure I'll be back at Christmas." He didn't push her away, nor did he hold her close. She was alone and, for the first time, terrified. She drew in a quick breath.

"I can't come back here after all the plans we've made. Tonight was torture for me——"

"As it was for me."

He grabbed her by her arms. "Was it? I don't want to be your casual friend. I want to be your husband. I won't settle for less."

"I understand." With all her might, she wanted to tell him she loved him, but that would give him hope, and she couldn't do that.

"Do you? Do you understand how you're killing me? And for what? Tell me what's wrong. What did I do? I'll fix it. Bloody hell, Rachel, I'll fix it." His anger broke over her like a crashing wave.

"No," she screamed. "You didn't do anything wrong. This isn't about you. It isn't even about us. This isn't what I want, but there's nothing either of us can do. There's nothing I can do. Mother needs me. I can't be here and in London. I can't be with you right now. Please, please, I need you to understand."

"Edythe looked fine tonight. Rachel, there's something you're not telling me. I don't know what it is or why you won't tell me. Your decision affects me, too."

His words battered her. She stood and took it. The seconds drew out to minutes as they faced each other. Silently, she pleaded her cause and knew he did the same.

"All right. I'll give you time. When you're ready for me to come back, leave a note in the tree." How would he know if she left a note in the tree? She let out a lifeless laugh at the irritation in his tone.

"I'll know it's there. I promise. There's no one else for me but you. Remember, I love you. My heart is yours—forever." He gently brought her into his arms and held her close.

The loud, strong pounding of his heart comforted her—a few more minutes. Please, don't leave. Just a little longer. *Her shoulders shook from silent tears.*

"Shush, don't cry. I don't know why you're doing this. I know you love me—" She raised her head to speak. "No, let me finish. No one else will ever love you as I do."

"Oh, Pryce, there's no one else. There's never been anyone for me but you. I just…" Her head returned to his chest. "I can't right now."

Her voice was a whisper. She squeezed her eyes tight, wanting to take back the words and the hurt, but couldn't. I love you, *she mouthed.*

The walk back to the house was long and lonely and without Pryce.

Every day she went to the oak tree with a note for him, *Meet me tonight. R,* only to return with it in her pocket. There was no use asking him to come back.

Days turned to weeks, and weeks turned to months. He was in London, doing great things, advancing quickly in the company. Proud of his achievements, she ached for him and cried for them both.

She wrote to him daily and waited for his letters until one day, two years later, there was nothing to write.

Chapter Six

Rachel's ability to ignore the discussion with Pryce for the rest of that evening amazed her. Their last evening together was perfect. He was perfect. Since then, his hurt expression had haunted her every day. When she walked by the oak tree, when she sat in her room, and when Rachel looked at her locket, his face was all she saw. Doubled over, head in her hands, she wept for both of them.

He didn't come home that Christmas or all of the following year. His business did well, he wrote in his letters. They made him a partner in record time. The year after that, nothing was left of them as a couple. The *Sommer Sentinel* reported on his successes. She read the notices with pride, sadness... and longing.

No longer able to deny the pain, she welcomed it, dared it to make her any more miserable. Wave after wave, memories consumed her, breaking down her controls, leaching out every emotion until she sat exposed. Empty and alone.

How many times had her lie returned to haunt her? She wanted to see Pryce one more time. Tell him the truth. He deserved that. *Truth, Rachel.* Only the truth, but was it for his benefit or for her peace of mind?

Would he even speak to her? A gasp rattled through her. Would he turn his back, walk away? She wouldn't blame him. Perhaps his denial would help move her forward instead of reliving, rethinking things that could never change.

What if he did see her? What would she say? What was her plan? Tell him that she knew he would stay if he knew the truth. He would give up the job he worked so hard to get and the future it promised. He'd understand that she couldn't hold him back, wouldn't he? Was that her plan? That she didn't think he was man enough to decide for himself. That he was a shallow, uncaring person, so rather than hear it from him, she'd made the decision.

The more she tried to ignore the truth, the more it persisted. Brenna had taught her well.

Her mother argued with her for weeks, months to tell him the truth, to trust him. Rachel refused. Nothing swayed her. Yet every day, she walked to the oak tree and weighed, asking him to come back. How headstrong and determined, and how wrong she had been.

No, she had no intention of planning her speech now. The last time she prepared a speech, it turned into a disaster. If Pryce did talk to her, she would speak from the heart.

She stared at the newspapers and sucked in a deep breath. *Return the papers to the trunk and wait for the party.* That was her plan.

With the article and folded papers in hand, she climbed the steps.

A cool breeze rustled her skirt when she reached the fourth floor. She glanced around the hall. Only the tower room door stood ajar.

Her brows wrinkled. Rachel stepped quietly into the room. The door to the witch's cap stood open. Someone stood on the walk, but with the bright sky in the background, she could only make out a dark silhouette. Her chest pounding, she moved into the shadows.

"I couldn't stay away. God knows I tried. I gave myself a hundred reasons not to be here. For years, I tried not to think of Sommer-by-the-Sea. I took on everything and anything to forget, to distance myself from here. But I couldn't.

"Besides, it's All Hallows Eve, and who can stay away? Everyone in England knows Emerson Manor is the place to be tonight. I was surprised when the Emersons approached the Historical Society to buy the house, but I'm glad they did. Some traditions should go on, and Edythe's masquerade party is one of them. They were always so much fun."

Storm clouds moved across the sky and momentarily blocked the sun.

"The times I spent here. The times I spent with you. You were always my biggest supporter." The shadow stiffened. "Even when I didn't deserve your loyalty. How do I ask you for forgiveness when I can't forgive myself?" The shadow slammed a hand on the wooden railing.

Rachel listened, well aware of who stood on the walk.

"You understood me better than I understood myself. And how did I repay you? By taking you for granted—no, it was worse than that. I didn't consider you at all. I knew you would always be there, no matter what I did or said."

And how different had Rachel treated Pryce? A tremble vibrated through Rachel like rolling thunder. It was just a different end of the spectrum. She saw that now.

The sun slipped out from behind the clouds. Beams of light blasted through the sky. One struck the oval window. The glare blinded Rachel. She shielded her eyes with her hand. Something spun in the glow. Tilting her head to the side to see what it was, she waited for the flash to fade. The cloud shifted, and Rachel stood mesmerized.

She blinked. Maybe it was the glare playing tricks on her. Another blink. It was still there. She reached out and poked it. Her locket dangled from the window's brass peg. She put the newspapers in the trunk and, in a daze, carefully removed the locket.

Her fingers traced the delicate filigree work and the cluster of small diamonds. She pried the locket open with great care and let out a small sigh. *My heart is yours—Forever.* She closed the locket and clutched it to her chest.

A sudden wave of keen emotion left her excited and thrilled. After so many years, it was hers once again. The golden heart was tied closely to Pryce's devotion—not only to her but also to them. The idea tempered her excitement, but now, more than ever, she needed to see Pryce. He must speak to her. If he objected, she'd make him talk to her.

In the doorway, the silhouette moved, and Rachel stepped back into the shadows near the hall door.

"You were so much the better person. And I did things… to hurt you. Terrible things." A choked laugh echoed in the room. "How many times did we have heart-to-heart talks? You were so sure you could save me. You tried so hard. But I couldn't be saved. Not then. I didn't think I was worth saving. I wish I knew why. My parents were loving, if a bit preoccupied. I had good friends, and most stood by me. I had no reason to strike out. Nothing stopped me until you left. That's when I realized. Well, it doesn't matter now."

Brenna stepped into the room, closed the door, and sat in the chair, her head in her hands.

Rachel stood in the shadows and put the locket around her neck.

"The last time I saw you, I took your locket. We were trying on clothes to wear to Mrs. Bainbridge's luncheon. I had just the dress to wear the locket with." Brenna shook her head. "No, that's only partially true. You wore the locket so proudly. Did you know I went with Pryce when he bought it for you? He was so particular about picking it out. The filigree had to be just right. The diamonds had to be placed just so. The inscription had to be perfect. He put so much love into that locket."

At first, Rachel didn't think she heard Brenna correctly. Even she had her suspicions. Brenna had been with her the night before the locket went missing. It was too much of a coincidence. Rachel was angry at Brenna for taking the locket and more so with herself for not confronting Brenna.

"I wanted to show the world that I was loved, too. Stupid, right? I thought you'd say so. I never wore it. I thought it would be blasphemous if I did. Each time I looked at it, my skin crawled with guilt. Taking your locket was a betrayal even I couldn't condone. It was as if the locket demanded I return it. Before I could give it back to you, Huntley dragged me to the Continent."

Brenna never hid her feelings about her relationship with Pryce, and after the birthday party incident, Rachel saw Brenna only in large groups or alone. Brenna often suggested double dating, but Pryce would have none of it. *Don't go looking for trouble*, he told her.

"Your parents had a good idea that I had the locket. Your father visited me in Italy for a heart-to-heart. Of course, Huntley was at the office. After a nice reunion of sorts, he startled me with his questions about the locket. I had the locket in my jewelry case and could've given it to him. Instead, I feigned being appalled at the accusation. I couldn't admit to him that I had the thing. I had to save face with him. Besides, you were the only one who would understand… even forgive me. We didn't return to Sommer-by-the-Sea for years, and by then, you were gone."

Her parents knew? She had been inconsolable.

"I treated Huntley as poorly as I treated you and pushed him right into the arms of one of his friend's wives. I blamed you. How vile is that? I blamed you for not being there for me. Me. Who was never there for you.

"I've kept the locket safe, but it's taken me two marriages to understand love needs to be earned, nurtured, and honored. I can apologize, make amends to everyone, but I can't face you. I'm sorry for so many things."

Brenna raised her head and looked around the room. "Remember how we played in here when we were children? Princess, pirate—even then, I took the role of the villain."

"Of course, I remember." Rachel stepped forward. "But I thought you wanted to be boss."

"I brought back—" Brenna turned toward the window, then shot out of the chair, letting out a loud gasp. Surprise drained the blood from her face.

"I miss you. Forgive me," Brenna whispered, then walked toward the door. She hesitated, a confused expression on her face.

Rachel stood next to her. "I forgive you."

Brenna's eyes widened, then she rushed down the stairs.

Rachel stood at the staircase. A few moments later, the echo of the front door closing reached her.

Chapter Seven

Rachel stepped back into the room. The sound of a carriage racing down the drive drew her to the window. The dust kicked up by the phaeton snaked down the drive and disappeared over the knoll. "I love you, Brenna. Sometimes I didn't like you, but I never stopped loving you."

Her mind spun from the day's emotional ups and downs, with memories of Pryce pure and clear. "Life's not always a smooth ride. Sometimes it's even stinky. You were so right, Father."

A long, exhausted sigh filled the room. There was no reason for Rachel to stay any longer. Her hand touched the locket at her throat. At last, everything was peace and contentment.

A smirk stretched across her face. Common sense told her to leave, the same common sense that let Pryce go.

See him from afar. That would satisfy her. Not talk to him or explain. Look at him one last time before she left. Maybe there would be no more torment at what could have been. She'd spent much too long doing that.

She glanced down at the drive. The house's lights reflected

in a shimmer on the damp ground. It would be a few hours before the party started.

Rachel plumped the chair cushions and tucked the blanket around her legs as her mother had done a hundred times. Comfortable and content, she watched the soft rain pelt the window and waited.

♥ ♥ ♥

Gravel flew as carriages drove up the drive from Manor Road, waking her from a light sleep. The evening sky was clear. The rain must have stopped hours ago. Rachel stretched and, on a whim, located Orion among the twinkling stars.

The window only let her see so much. They should put the lights on around the house. Mother always lit the house and grounds like a Christmas tree.

Without a good view of the activities, Rachel folded the blanket. She reached for her throat, then relaxed. Her locket was still in place. Intent on gathering every memory, she scanned the room, knowing this would be her last time here. Satisfied and ready, she moved down the stairs to the second floor.

From her vantage point, looking over the balcony railing, people ran, crisscrossing the Great Hall. The footmen, dressed in white shirts under black suits, transformed into skeletons with white-and-black makeup and placed drinks on the table around the large vase. Someone else followed behind, dropping cubes into the glasses.

Ina, dressed in a lovely ball gown, came into view. "Someone get to the kitchen and help set the trays on the buffet tables. Put the coats in the green room. It's that door on the right."

"People are here from the London Times and Sommer Sentinel," one of the volunteers said.

"Show them to the ballroom. Let me know when you see the mayor, council, and the Historical Society. They should be here for an interview in about fifteen minutes. I don't know how Brenna Hutchington accomplished that. Her connections are amazing. Come with me. I want to see if the people from the newspaper need any help." Ina and two people dressed as ghosts went into the ballroom.

A Tudor princess and a Viking charged across the floor below. A moment later, two nurses and a pirate came into view, carrying boxes. There were dominoes, vampires, and even a Queen of England. The musicians started.

As she knew, sitting in the balcony had its advantages. You heard every conversation.

"Mr. Mayor, Mr. Washburn, Lady Hutchington, this way, please." A vampire ushered the people into the Great Hall.

"Brenna, thank you for hosting dinner."

"I'd like to thank the newest member of the House of Commons, Mr. Washburn, for joining us…" Brenna started to say.

"Not quite yet. We'll see the results soon."

This man must be Evan Washburn, Sommer-by-the-Sea's hero. Evan had grown into quite a man. The woman she'd met walking the terrier was with him. They both wore pirate costumes. Rachel gasped. Evan wore a real wooden pirate leg.

"Clever costume, Evan. You wear your badge of courage well. I can't help but thank you for serving and keeping us safe." Brenna's words struck Rachel. Not what she said, but the sincerity of them.

"You're familiar with the house?" Mrs. Henry, the mayor's wife, asked Brenna. Ina joined them.

"Yes, the Emersons have been close friends since childhood," Brenna said.

"Sorry to interrupt, but they need you in the ballroom." Ina stepped up next to them.

The others went on. Ina held Brenna back. "Your Gypsy costume is wonderful. Are you competing with our fortune teller?"

"No," she laughed. "I'm very happy with not knowing the future."

"I wanted to thank you for arranging the interview. Everyone's excited."

"I know the company's general counsel in London. I mentioned the event and spoke to a few people. Keep close to her."

"I'll make sure to get her information and send a thank-you note next week." Ina wrote herself a note.

"By the way, I noticed you don't have all the lights on outside the house. You may want to put them on."

"They should have been put on. I'll check. You go on to the others. I'll be there shortly."

Brenna stared up at the balcony, a question on her face.

Rachel drew closer to the rail. "You still have my India earrings. The ones my father gave me," she mumbled.

Brenna touched her ear, shook her head, and entered the ballroom.

"Ina." A volunteer ran in from the entrance carrying a large box. "There's a skunk outside, and people waiting to enter are getting nervous. Can we let them in? It's only fifteen minutes until the doors open."

"Skunk? Ah, that's why Brenna reminded me about the lights. Put on all the outside lights, even the ones that line the drive down to Manor Road. That should keep the critters away. The last thing we need is our quests sprayed by a skunk. Let them in, but only if they're wearing a costume. No costume—hand them one of the masks." Ina pointed to the box.

The Great Hall was the only way to the ballroom. Rachel's perch on the balcony provided a perfect view of every guest. The doors to the ballroom were open, and music filtered out. It didn't appear to bother anyone.

The party was underway when the grand clock struck ten. There was only a trickle of newcomers now.

By eleven, the volunteers joined the party. One hour. Had he gotten past her in the crush of guests? He had to be here. It was a masquerade party. He wouldn't stay away. She wound her arms around herself and tried to stop the building ache.

No sense staying here. Rachel came down the stairs. She wasn't in a costume and looked in the box for a mask. It was empty. That wasn't going to stop her. Desperate to find him, she walked up to and looked at every man. They must have thought her crazy, but that didn't matter. They ignored her and kept talking over the music.

She had been through most of the room and stood at one of the tables to gather her thoughts. No, to push down the building panic.

"I'll have one of those," the woman who stood at the table with her said to the passing footman. To Rachel's surprise, it was the woman with the purple scarf.

"Excuse me—" Rachel said.

"Tanya, I've been looking for you." Rachel turned and looked at a woman in a Russian Snow Queen costume. "Come with me back to the bar. The mayor's wife is waiting for you to read her tea leaves." The two women rushed to the bar.

The clock struck the half hour. It was eleven thirty.

"Can I have everyone's attention, please?" Rachel turned. Brenna stood in the middle of the room.

"I'd like to thank everyone for coming to the Duchess of Harrington's Masquerade Ball. The judges will announce the costume contest winners in a few moments. Personally, I think the pirate serving drinks is… well, maybe I shouldn't say." A roll of laughter went through the room.

"This house is very special to me. I played here with my dearest friend and have many wonderful memories. This was a happy house. After a great deal of discussion, the Sommer-by-the-Sea Historical Society, in conjunction with the Emerson Foundation, has decided to continue to restore Emerson Manor to its original grandeur. It will be a place to learn about life and art during the different eras that it was an active home for the Emersons.

"One year ago, the Emerson Foundation gave us a challenge. They would match donations raised by the village pound for pound. The Fund has reached a milestone, five million dollars." Everyone applauded. "At midnight, we have some surprises for you when we finalize the transfer of this beautiful manor to the Historical Society.

"As this year's committee chairwoman, I'd like to thank all our volunteers. Here is Mayor Henry, who will announce the winners of the costume contests."

The clock struck the quarter hour, a quarter to twelve.

Rachel looked frantically from one face to another. It was close to midnight. No, Pryce. Her breath came in short spurts as the realization hit her hard. He wasn't coming. It was a childish notion, and life didn't happen that way. Rachel knew that better than most, but she had been so sure.

Crowded by the closeness of the ballroom, hollow and empty at not seeing Pryce, her time had run out. She hurried into the garden as the party approached the witching hour, and the guests filtered out to watch the fireworks.

She sped through the garden, rushed to the back, turned at the dogleg, and came to a screeching halt. The manor lights weren't on here. Out of breath, Rachel stared at the oak tree shrouded in darkness against the halo of lights from the village in the distance.

This was her place. Rachel didn't need lights to find her way. Maybe Pryce never got her note. She ran to the oak tree and searched the knothole. It wasn't there. Falling to her knees, she scoured the ground and wildly sifted through the leaves. The note had to be here. Nothing.

"I wasn't sure you'd come." A male voice pinned her to the spot.

With a start, Rachel stood up, her eyes shut, a gentle sob escaping from her throat. *Thank you.*

"Rachel?" His voice was mellow and soft, better than she remembered. He came around and faced her.

"Pryce." Her heart slammed into her chest at seeing him until she thought she would burst.

Somewhere a clock began to strike midnight. Pryce took her hand, and they walked to the other side of the fence, near the Emerson family grave site.

"Rachel, do you love me?" She looked into his eyes and saw the passion she remembered, the passion in her dreams. It hadn't faded. He didn't hate her.

"I never stopped," she whispered. The clock continued to strike the hour.

She rushed into his open arms. They were warm, protecting, and, oh, God's teeth, loving. "I have something to tell you."

"Not now. No talking now. I want to hold you. I've waited so long." He cupped her head and drew her to his chest.

"No." She pushed away. "I've kept this secret from you too long. You've always been honest. But I've… I've lied to you."

He waited for her to continue, his face open and encouraging. The clock struck again.

"I was ill, not Mother. There was no hope." Her voice trailed off to a whisper. Time had not eased that pain. "I sent you away because I knew you loved me and would never leave me, and your life would be much different if you had stayed. I would have cost you your job and your future."

"The decision wasn't yours to make alone. There were two of us in the relationship, and we should have had an equal say."

"Yes, you're right, but I knew what you'd do. I didn't want to be a burden. More than that, I couldn't stand it if your love turned to hate."

"Did you think me that shallow? My love for you so—"

"No. I was the coward. I know that now. For days, something compelled me to come here today."

"I've spent the day at the manor, going over events and decisions. I made a terrible mistake. I never doubted you. Not for a minute. I thought I knew best." Another tone from the clock.

He held her. "I know what you thought. Now it's time for me to confess. I have a secret that I've held from you. I knew that you were ill, not your mother. I sat down with your parents the day after your mother's party. They didn't want to discuss it, but I played every card I had and forced them to tell me the truth. I wasn't leaving until they did. They made me promise not to mention anything to you unless you told me yourself."

She cried for the months and years of happiness they could have had. For the comfort they could have given each other. For the love they could have shared—the clock's eighth strike of the hour.

"The hardest thing I've ever done was honor that request. I visited your mother every week. When she told me you were too weak to write and you were failing, I came to you. Even though you didn't recognize me, I never left your side. And I made you a promise."

They both looked at the grave in front of them.

Lady Rachel Emerson
December 19, 1789, to January 24, 1815
Beloved Daughter and Pryce's Fiancée

"I remember." Her fingers touched the delicate locket around her neck. "My heart is yours—Forever." The ninth beat of the clock.

"It just took me a little longer to join you." He stood to the side and exposed the newly dug grave.

Pryce Drake, Earl Somerset
May 25, 1787, to October 25, 1829.
With Rachel at Last.

"One week ago," she said in a tone filled with awe. "How?"

"It was a heart attack. Your mother was with me. She told me to be here at midnight. She's a mighty witch."

Pryce looked over his shoulder at the oak. She followed his gaze. Her breath caught. Rachel stared into warm, loving eyes.

"Mother. Father," she whispered.

I told you you'd find your locket. Rachel's mother's soft, warm tones echoed in her head. It was her voice. Her mother had been with her all along.

Her parents stood at the oak tree, her mother dressed in a witch's costume and her father in his dinner attire.

"Come, Edythe. It's time to go. You've done all you can for both of them." Her father looked at them. "Keep her safe, Pryce. And Princess, save a waltz for me." He wiped his eyes and put his arm around Edythe.

Her mother blew Rachel a kiss. Her parents stood there a moment, then turned and walked back to the manor.

Pryce turned her to face him as the mist surrounded them. His gaze was a soft caress. Instinctively and with great yearning, she stepped closer to him and playfully sniffed.

"No skunk," he said. The warmth of his smile echoed in his voice.

He was all she wanted, all she had thought about. The connection was immediate as if the lost years never happened. They belonged together. She knew that now. Every part of her body screamed for him.

His hands slipped up her arms and brought her close.

She couldn't get close enough. She fought to control the building excitement that his touch ignited but quickly relented.

With a bent finger, he raised her chin and lowered his lips a breath away from hers. Her body was on fire, with a liquid heat concentrated between her thighs. She gasped at the sweet agony. He gathered her closer in his arms—the eleventh strike of the hour.

Nervously, she wet her lips. Pryce's chest rumbled with a deep groan. The touch of his mouth on hers sent a tremor through her. He tempted her with his tongue and teased her mouth open. Breathless, she hesitated only a moment. He swooped in, and she let him claim her mouth and quivered at the sweet tenderness of his kiss. Every nerve was alive. Every touch of his lips made her dizzy with delight.

He kissed her cheek lightly, then worked his way to her earlobe. His warm breath sent chills all through her. She sank into his arms.

"Forever," he moaned.

A sense of urgency drove her. The dizzying current raced through her as the wind picked up, sending the dried leaves around them. The more the wind blew, the more insistent the urgency became. In Pryce's arms, her guilt faded until only love remained.

With one last gust of wind, on the final stroke of midnight, the witching hour, Pryce led her away at the first burst of fireworks.

They went on together to their eternity of happy ever afters.

Thank you for taking the time to read The Lady and Her Secret (The Return to the Ladies of Sommer-by-the-Sea, Book 4). And thank you in advance for sharing your enjoyment of this story (or my other stories) with fellow readers by leaving a review on Amazon. Long or short, detailed or to the point, I read all the reviews and greatly appreciate you for writing one!

To keep up to date with new stories, where you can find me, and my friends, please consider subscribing to my newsletter (and receive a free book as a gift)

Excerpt

The Lady and Her Quill

Lady Alicia Hartley's head kept telling her to stop loving him,
but her heart couldn't let him go.

"It's very easy to get involved with our characters feelings in
this historical romance. Both are right and wrong, and when
they realize that the excitement and adventure really starts."
~ Petula, Goodreads, 5 Stars

Renowned author Lady Alicia Hartley has lost her muse
after a bad review. She blames it all on the author JC Melrose.
A chance encounter with a handsome, witty Justin Caulfield has
her heart racing, and her muse seemingly back. Is he her savior
or her worst nightmare?

The recently retired Captain Justin Caulfield is facing his
own demons. As gifted author JC Melrose, his stories honor
men who died at the hand of one man. His only focus is to

avenge their deaths, that is, until he meets and falls in love with Lady Alicia.

The two authors take on a writing challenge based on a story of stolen gold taken from the newspaper headlines all to determine the better writer. While researching the story, Lady Alicia is captured by the thieves' ringleader. Can Lady Alicia turn this mystery into an award-winning story? Can Justin save his real-life heroine? Can they both overcome their own challenges for a happily ever after?

Chapter One

Lady Alicia Hartley clutched the heavy parcel under her arm and hurried along Fleet Street through the thick fog. She took scant notice of the people rushing past her or the church bells chiming noon. New ideas fluttered and flittered through her mind. Success had led to opportunities she never dreamt possible until now. Her lips pursed as she tried to suppress a satisfied smile.

Caution. The small inner voice broke through her dreaming and her brows knitted together. Don't be reckless.

Alicia rubbed the amber stone she wore around her neck. The pendant was a gift from her father.

Confidence is everything, though, was one of Mrs. Bainbridge's guiding principles.

It started with Miss Whitlock. Since Alicia was a little girl, Miss Greta Whitlock had been her governess. Alicia was fond of the tall, pleasant woman who at times was more like an older sister. Some of her best memories were sitting in the window seat in the attic room, staring at the sea and just talking about hopes, aspirations, dreams, and well, everything. Nothing was prohibited. If anything, the woman encouraged her to be an independent thinker and draw her own conclusions.

Alicia soon became proficient in drawing, needlecraft, music, and dance. While only a passing knowledge of French and Italian was expected, Alicia excelled past songs and snippets of poems and stories presented in the romantic languages. Her natural curiosity eventually drove her to acquire fluency in both, and proficiency in Greek and Latin.

Her schooling included the practical study of household management that went beyond managing the staff and counting the silver, but also included training in hiring, purchasing, and gardening.

Decorum ruled a lady's life from her core to her habits. Nothing less was tolerated. Everything she did was scrutinized and criticized, but Miss Whitlock had done her job well.

They spent hours in the attic at her desk and looked forward to those days her father was not home. He agreed she could use his library when it wasn't occupied. She sat at the large table, surrounded by books, and enjoyed their sweet, musky scent.

Of all the subjects, her true love was writing – taking the actions, colors, sounds, and emotions of imaginary people and places she conjured in her mind and translating them into words for others to read and enjoy.

She had all but driven Miss Whitlock dizzy with her thirst for knowledge and her quest to improve her writing.

By the time she was fifteen, she mastered all the acceptable subjects a young woman was expected to learn and others some people would think unnecessary, a waste of time, or worse, scandalous.

With her parents' agreement, her governess sometimes submitted her essays to the village paper, the Sommer Sentinel.

Mr. Leon Hawkins, the elderly owner, enjoyed her short story about Margaret's Miracle, a long-held folk tale about the village mayor's daughter Margaret and a Scottish trader. It was a reflective essay that spoke about the tale and introduced ideas based on facts she researched.

Hawkins also printed her more creative pieces. One in particular, her story that featured an upper-class lady and her plight in London society, had been very well received.

"You make me proud," Miss Whitlock had said, standing next to her at the library table, her hands clasped in front of her.

Proud. Alicia glowed brighter than the light from the oil lamp at the compliment.

"Put your books away and bundle up. It's bitterly cold out, and we're going to the tearoom today."

It was an innocent excursion. One they had made many times before. One she thoroughly enjoyed. Or was it the biscuits that drew her there?

When they arrived at the tearoom, Miss Whitlock led the way to a table by the window, where they joined another woman.

"Honoria, I'd like to introduce you to Lady Alicia Hartley." Miss Whitlock turned to her.

"Lady Alicia, this is my dear friend, Mrs. Honoria Bainbridge."

Everyone knew Mrs. Bainbridge — if not in person, then most definitely by reputation. She was the head of the Sommer-by-the-Sea Female Seminary, an elite school that every girl in the district, if not all of England, wanted to attend.

One didn't apply to the seminary. Admittance was only by Mrs. Bainbridge's personal invitation.

She and Miss Whitlock took their seats. Tea was already laid and waiting for them. At first, Alicia thought she would be a silent observer and given an opportunity to occasionally add her voice to the conversation.

Instead, she sat at the table as if she was a pane of glass, one both women saw right through. As tea progressed, she became anxious, and she had no idea why.

"Lady Alicia." Pulled from her star-gazing, she faced Mrs. Bainbridge. "Have you seen the London papers? Edmund Kean has signed a contract with Drury Lane. He is to play Shylock in The Merchant of Venice. They are expecting a comedy," Mrs. Bainbridge said as she picked up her teacup. "What do you think of the play?"

It was a straightforward question.

One she was prepared for. She had studied Shakespeare and knew the play. "To me, the play is a drama, especially when Portia, disguised as a lawyer, begs Shylock to show mercy to Antonio. Her speech on the quality of mercy is dramatic and moving." Alicia took a breath and leaned forward, eager to go on. "The characters are sensitive and engaging. I don't see this play as a comedy. Although, I do think there are scenes where Shakespeare inserts comic elements to provide relief for the story's tension. But is the play a comedy? Not to me."

Mrs. Bainbridge smiled and gazed at her thoughtfully, then turned to Miss Whitlock.

"With the cold temperatures this last month, the Thames has frozen. There are plans for a frost fair between Blackfriars Bridge and London Bridge on the first of February." Mrs. Bainbridge set down her teacup and sighed. "I was a little girl when they had the last one."

Alicia really didn't want to talk about Shakespeare or the frost fair. She stared out the window at the cold gray sky and willed herself to stay in her seat.

"I read your story in the Sommer Sentinel."

Alicia whipped her head around and again faced Mrs. Bainbridge.

"Your story, the experience of a young upper-class woman who must navigate London society for the first time and falls in love with a social superior, was very good. I thoroughly enjoyed the way you re-created the social world. Your characters are sensitive and engaging. I like the way you let your reader experience their distress and tenderness.

"The conflict is well-planned and given with enough context to maintain a good pace and keep your reader turning pages. You are a good storyteller."

Alicia felt her face flush at the compliment. "Thank you, Mrs. Bainbridge. I'm glad you enjoyed the story."

"I do see room for growth."

Alicia stared at the woman and tamped down her annoyance. What was wrong with her writing?

She didn't think the headmistress would wait long to tell her.

"Draw out the conversations. Just because you know where it is going does not mean your reader does. And give a little more exposition within the narrative itself as an anchor."

"It is very kind of you to give me some direction. I will certainly keep your comments in mind."

"I expect you will. I see a young person eager to succeed. You will, you know. You are a gifted storyteller."

Mrs. Bainbridge gave her a smile, not one of those smiles that didn't reach the eyes, but a smile that came from her heart.

Alicia took a biscuit and finished her tea. She gave Miss Whitlock a fleeting glance. Her governess sat proudly by as she engaged in a conversation with Mrs. Bainbridge.

She liked her governess, but she wanted to learn more. In truth, she longed to be under Mrs. Bainbridge's tutelage. The headmistress worked with her students to create a plan filled with courses that surpassed anything Miss Whitlock could teach. Some were usually only available to men.

Mrs. Bainbridge's words kept repeating in her head.

You are a gifted storyteller.

With tea over and the snow beginning to fall, they said their good-byes and departed.

"What do you think of Mrs. Bainbridge?" Miss Whitlock asked as they walked along the river.

"She's an excellent judge of writing talent."

Miss Whitlock stared at her for a heartbeat or two before she burst out laughing. "Yes, she is," she concluded. "And I think she gave you excellent advice."

Mr. Dodd, the butler, opened the door as they reached it.

Alicia and Miss Whitlock went into the drawing room, laughing like schoolgirls. The soft scent of violet on the air announced her mother was present.

"Did you have a nice outing?" Lady Hartley said, looking over her spectacles as she stitched a sampler.

"It was wonderful. We had tea with Mrs. Bainbridge. And I was careful, I didn't spill my cup and I only took one biscuit."

Lady Hartley smiled and put down her stitching. "Yes, I know you can be quite civil when you put your mind to it."

"Mrs. Bainbridge complimented me on my essay that was in the Sentinel."

"Then she must have good literary taste," her mother said. "Before I forget, you received a letter."

"It must be from Hattie in London. She told me she'd write to tell me when she was returning to Sommer-by-the-Sea." Alicia took the dispatch from the salver and opened the letter.

She took a seat next to her mother, read the contents, then stared at the note without saying a word.

"Alicia, is anything wrong? I've never seen you so quiet," her mother said, glancing at Miss Whitlock.

Alicia looked at her governess, then her mother.

"What is it?" her mother asked.

"It's an invitation." Her heart was beating so loud she was sure her mother could hear it. She lifted her chin. "Mrs. Bainbridge has invited me to be a student at the Sommer-by-the-Sea Female Seminary."

Looking back, she had no idea that tea with Mrs. Bainbridge would change her life. That was seven years ago. She spent five wonderful years at the Sommer Female Seminary learning everything she could. Now, two years later, she still heard Mrs. Bainbridge's words warning caution.

She clutched the parcel to her chest. This completed project was a good one. Better than her last. As soon as she presented it to Mr. Caulfield, he too would be enthusiastic.

Remain calm. Be gracious and pleasant but remain firm.

By the time she had mentally repeated the words several times, her doubts quieted. Of course, Caulfield would bargain. She would remind him their past achievements were for the most part her doing. She no longer wanted to sell her story to Caulfield Publishing for a fee and receive nothing beyond that. Her books sold well and made a profit, but only for Caulfield.

The sales gave her the confidence to ask for a change in their financial arrangement on this last book in her contract. She would gladly pay all the production costs for publication. Caulfield Publishing would distribute them and get ten percent from the profits, a reasonable and more equitable financial arrangement. It would also give her more control of her work. She pressed her parcel closer to her chest. If he wouldn't budge, there was the letter that arrived in yesterday's post.

How could he refuse?

Her smile dropped and her step faltered. Question her project, perhaps, but refuse? He couldn't. He wouldn't. Would he? A cold chill that had nothing to do with the weather ran up her spine.

A passing carriage startled her, shaking her out of her moment of distraction. Alicia looked about. Temple Church was to her right. Her destination wasn't much further. She resumed walking, but at a slower pace.

What if he did not agree to her request? She stared at the ground as if by some miracle the answer lay at her feet.

"I admire your conviction, Alicia, but you can't always have your way. In all things there is a give and take, a bargaining. Coming to a mutual understanding is the way both you and the other person will be successful."

More wisdom from Mrs. Bainbridge. The woman had an uncanny way of always seeing the truth of a matter.

It would be best for her to be prepared to listen, then bargain. See a way for both she and Mr. Caulfield to come away a winner. Satisfied she had a plan, she quickened her step, eager to come to an agreement with her publisher and present him with her finished manuscript. She crossed Fetter Lane and came to her destination, Number 32.

Alicia entered the building, climbed the stairs, and stood at the door to Caulfield Publishing. Isaac Caulfield was a congenial gentleman for the most part, but occasionally he acted like most men—opinionated, closed-minded, and unrelenting.

Caulfield Publishing was not the first publisher she approached. She had set her sights on the renowned William Lane. With grace, he declined her manuscript and advised her the best and probably only way her story would be published was if she paid to have it printed and sold copies to her family and friends.

As an afterthought, he suggested a small, unknown company, Caufield Publishing.

She returned home heartbroken. Her sister, Beatrice, and brother-in-law, Captain Douglas Elkington, tried to soothe her. She told them Mr. Lane suggested another publisher, one more willing to produce her type of story. It was Elkington's approval that made her consider the idea. Intent and undeterred, she approached Isaac Caulfield.

He was not enthusiastic when she brought him her first manuscript.

Not at all.

He was ready to reject her story before he read a single word. Desperate, she cajoled him into reading the piece before he passed judgement.

That was two years ago. Now, their business arrangement was a successful one. Earlier this week Caulfield released and sent her fifth book, The Lost Dowry, to the library on Leadenhall Street.

Her triumphs were on her side.

Alicia took a deep breath, straightened her spine, turned the latch, and entered. "Good day, Mr. Caulfield."

The publisher sprang to his feet.

"Lady Alicia." He pulled out his pocket watch. "You're early. What a pleasant surprise. Please, be seated."

"I apologize for my early arrival, but I am eager to speak with you."

"Are you here alone?" He came to her side and glanced out the door.

"Yes." She winced at the trace of defiance in her voice. Another social blunder. Beatrice warned her London propriety was different from that at home in Sommer-by-the-Sea. It amazed her that a different world existed three hundred miles south of the village.

A chaperone.

The idea made her teeth itch. Today, Beatrice was otherwise engaged and in truth, Alicia's patience ran thin waiting for her.

She stepped inside. The office was cramped not because it was small, but because it was in disarray. Everywhere she looked, there were books and papers. Dark walnut bookcases stuffed with unorderly books lined the left side of the room. Light filtered through bedraggled curtains on the large windows to her right. Several stacks of papers filled Mr. Caulfield's desk, which was positioned in front of the window. Similar bookshelves were on either side of the fireplace on the far wall

— but were hidden behind a pile of papers on a second desk across from Caulfield's. The clutter of papers and books rendered that desk unusable. A modest fire burned in the grate to take off the chill.

She was surprised the entire place didn't go up in flames.

She stepped with care around crates that littered the floor, removed the London Gazette laying on the chair, and settled into the seat.

"My sister was unavailable to join us. She and her husband are preparing the family for a trip north to join our parents for the village's Harvest Festival. I wanted to speak to you before we left."

Had he heard her? She followed his stare. He was focused on the Gazette in her hand. She glanced at his desk, the chair next to her, but there was no place to put it.

"I'm leaving with the family for Sommer-by-the-Sea. I look forward to reading at Mrs. Miller's Circulating Library. I wanted to thank you for seeing that my books were delivered."

"You're most welcome. I'm sure reading small segments of your story will encourage people to either borrow or buy your book. I am glad you're here. I wanted to speak to you today on another subject. I too, will be leaving London." He reached for the Gazette. "Here. Let me have the newspaper, if you please."

Alicia took a quick look at the headline: Missing Walmer Castle Chest Found – Empty?

She glanced at Caulfield's extended hand. She was about to give the newspaper to him when she spotted a corner of the paper was turned down, exposing the book review page. She opened the paper and stopped.

One review was circled: The Lost Dowry.

She read the article out loud.

"This is the fifth little story by Lady Alicia Hartley. While her other stories held promise, this book does not reach the standards the author established in her previous publications.

Perhaps the author's muse has gone astray. The characters and conflicts in The Lost Dowry had potential but only the heroine, who is quite good, shines. It is unfortunate that the others appear to have lost their way. They are forced, mechanical, and obstruct the story. In a word, they are disappointing. In this story..."

Skipping the summary of the plot, she went to the final paragraph.

"She should read J. C. Melrose's In My Brother's Shadow or any of the other eight stories in that series. There is an author who evokes a man's emotion, albeit the author could use some assistance with the female point of view. Can you imagine if these authors combined their skills? They would lay out a plot with characters that would keep you reading until the last page or the last flicker of your candle."

The newspaper trembled in her hand. She went back to the beginning of the article to find the name of the reviewer. Anonymous.

The coward.

Her eyes focused on the review. The small quakes and quivers of the paper she held attested to the state of her nerves.

"How did an appraisal of my story turn into a review for…" Her words clipped, her tone chilly, she spoke with as reasonable a voice as she could manage and scanned the article. "J. C. Melrose?"

She lowered the paper. Mr. Caulfield's lips moved as the empty feeling in her stomach built into a furious storm. She wasn't aware of anything he said, until his words filtered through at last.

"Lady Hartley, are you listening? Reviews like this are…not unusual. Keep in mind, you can't please every reader. I'm glad to publish your little stories."

"Little stories." Her heart galloped like a horse in the steeple chase. Her hand touched her pendant. Remain calm.

But soothing herself was getting more difficult by the moment. Even rubbing her stone didn't help now.

People were buying her novels, all of them. Alicia thrust the offensive paper at him.

"Perhaps we should give the readers some time. We plan to publish your next story in the summer. I want to speak to you about my plans for the company. I've bought a new press—"

"The plan was for my new story to be published in February. Now you want a delay? Or do you mean to cancel our agreement?"

His face closed, as if guarding a secret. Her heart sank. He accepted this review. He may be tolerating her tirade, but he agreed with Anonymous.

Unable to remain calm a moment longer, she shot him a penetrating glare as she rose, her parcel in hand.

"Not at all." He sprang to his feet, his chair scraping the floor behind him. "Being an author is not easy, Lady Alicia. I warned you before we began you would be at the mercy of the reading public, a capricious lot. I knew you were persistent and had promise." He studied her over the rim of his glasses. "I believe you still do, but with the new press I have plans to—"

But.

How often had she heard that insignificant word in front of every variation of the word no, a weapon men used to deny a woman her due?

"This is one review." Alicia paced the small space in front of his desk. "Caulfield Publishing has published five of my," she turned and faced him, "'little stories' to your financial advantage."

He gave her a sheepish glance.

"Before I let you read this…" She paused and held up her parcel. "I'll give your suggestion to delay publishing more thought, then send you my decision."

As disappointment and despair dimmed her enthusiasm, she questioned what happened to yesterday's excitement and celebration. The Lost Dowry was in the circulating library. Congratulatory notes from friends were piled on the salver on the foyer table.

And there was the letter.

She couldn't believe her good fortune when she read William Lane's message, although Elkington believed it. She had never seen her brother-in-law so excited. He took out the sherry and they all toasted the occasion. But now…her dream was dissolving in front of her eyes.

How could one awful review ruin everything? Mr. Lane would not want to read her manuscript now, and Mr. Caulfield questioned publishing her next story. Remaining calm was out of the question.

Her secret was out. She had done a good job and convinced herself and everyone else Lady Alicia Hartley was an author.

Everyone but one reviewer. Her breath came in small bursts. She stared at the Gazette on his desk and wanted to tear it to pieces.

"Lady Alicia, please sit down. We'll discuss this and come to a decision that is satisfactory to us both."

She glanced at the man, remained motionless, and held her words behind her teeth, not trusting herself to speak. Afraid she'd say something she would regret, Alicia turned and marched to the door with as much dignity as possible.

"My 'little stories,' as you like to refer to them, are all the rage."

She grabbed the latch and hoped he didn't observe her trembling hand or her watery eyes. At the moment, her single thought was to escape.

"Please, come sit and we can discuss our course of action without any—"

"Womanly emotions?" Her voice was heavy with sarcasm.

"No, not at all. I've been trying to tell you about some changes."

"Another time, perhaps. My family is traveling north, and I mustn't delay." By all that was holy, she needed to get away from the man.

"I understand. My regards to your sister and brother-in-law." He called to her as she pulled open the door and collided into a solid obstacle. Startled and thrown off balance, Alicia lost her grip on her parcel and sent the bundle tumbling to the floor.

Strong hands grasped her shoulders to steady her. Alicia's head snapped up. She stared into concerned gray, silver-streaked eyes. She took a deep breath and was surprised by the scent of lavender and citrus.

"I... I... forgive me, sir." She lowered her gaze to the gloved hand on her right shoulder and back to his penetrating stare. "Release me, please. I assure you I have recovered."

The man's concerned expression vanished, replaced with a humorous glint. He removed his hands and stepped away.

His great coat flowed around him as he bent and retrieved her parcel from the floor. Her shoulders felt the ghost of his strong yet gentle grasp. As he stood, she looked away eager to leave.

"There is nothing to forgive." He bent his head toward her and handed her the bundle. "I, too, would want to make a fast escape from Mr. Caulfield."

"Thank you," she said without any humor, pulling the parcel close.

"My pleasure, I assure you." The gentleman tipped the brim of his hat.

Alicia turned and rushed down the stairs.

♥ ♥ ♥

Justin Caulfield entered his uncle's office. He glanced around, but found no place for his hat. He settled on putting it on the stack of books on the mantel.

"Lady Alicia is a determined woman." Isaac went to the grate for a taper to light his pipe. "And she was correct."

So, that was the illustrious Lady Alicia Hartley. Ever since his uncle shared the accounts with him, he'd been going on and on about the woman and her so-called little stories. That the man was distressed was an understatement. What had upset him and his treasured author?

"Correct? What do you mean?"

"She is correct that her stories generate a considerable amount of money for the company. I won't lose her. Her reaction to that review surprised me." His uncle pointed to the paper. "She's received other reviews that have not been favorable. But this one upset her."

Justin picked up the London Gazette.

"Don't blame yourself. She would have read or heard about this in due course." He tossed the paper onto the desk without reading the review. "We both are aware reviews are subjective. An author will not please everyone. Did you get my message?" His uncle asked, then looked up at him.

"I found it when I arrived last night. I'm going to visit Lord Barrington in Sommer-by-the-Sea and will make your delivery for you. How did your favorite author react when you told her you were retiring to the country, and a new publisher and editor was taking your place?" Justin leaned over the desk and searched through the papers in the in-basket.

"I tried more than once to tell her my plan, but the woman didn't give me the opportunity."

Justin, still bent over the basket, stopped his search and glanced at his uncle.

"You didn't tell her."

"Her new manuscript was in that parcel. But she was like a dog with a bone and wouldn't let go of the review. I suggested we publish the story later in the year, perhaps this summer."

Justin straightened and put down the papers that were in his hand. "Let me guess. That's when she rose to her feet and stormed out."

"Near weeping. I prayed she would keep them at bay. I can't abide a woman's tears. I'm certain she doubts my confidence in her writing. But I assure you, I'm quite convinced of her ability. I wanted to inform her of our plans for the company. About you stepping in, but the Gazette review held her full attention." The man leaned forward with his face flushed in anger. "A dog with a bone, I tell you."

"Now, now. There is no need to get upset. She is emotional and will come around if she wants her next story published."

"My intent to delay publishing her story had nothing to do with that… that article." He pointed to the Gazette. "I wanted the new publisher, you, to work with her on her story."

"It's not easy listening to criticism of your work." He held papers in his hand and stared at the desk. A heartbeat later, he let out an exasperated sigh and returned to his search. "I know. I've had my share of disappointing reviews. Whether I work with her or not, I don't agree with you putting off her publication date. If anything, I would publish her next story ahead of schedule. Releasing a new book close to this review may be to your advantage. If the review is as bad as you say, a new release could encourage curiosity."

"That may not be a bad idea." His uncle sat back in his chair. The flush subsided from his face. "I leave the decision up to you and her."

"You're not out the door yet."

"No. I'll always be close. But dealing with creative people is not easy. Their work is an integral part of them, and at times they are not able to separate their story from themselves. Like the reviewer has his bias, the author has theirs. To them, their work is perfect. Take your writing."

"My writing? I thought you enjoyed my stories. I write big

ones, not little ones." He teased his uncle. He was halfway through the pile.

"I do enjoy your stories. Big or little, they are excellent. Your understanding of soldiers and the battlefield are exceptional. It's no surprise to me that Lord Barrington and the Duke of Wellington call on you even though you are no longer in the service. You're the epitome of a fine Highland warrior."

Justin, with one eyebrow raised, gave him a sideways glance. "Me? A fine Highland warrior. You've been reading too much Walter Scott." He returned to looking through the papers.

"You mock me? Well, I'm not surprised. You always did underestimate your abilities. Put you in a kilt with a claymore in your hand, and your bloodline will show. It did on the battlefield. You were fierce – a force few men wanted to cross. But it is much more than your broad chest and handsome knees. There is another side to the Justin Caulfield I know."

"And what is that other side?" he asked, chuckling, still digging through the pile of papers.

"There is a very human side to you. I remember the rambunctious lad who filched tarts from the kitchen, ran the fields with his friends, and stood up to those who thought to bully him. You weren't fast to take to your fists, no. You tried to settle things with words. But when needed, you stood up for yourself and others. You never backed down. You've grown to understand what drives people. You don't abuse it, but rather, you help them to be their best. It is what makes you a good leader… and you bring all that knowledge and expertise to your stories. However, even they have room for improvement." His uncle glanced briefly at the door. "You could learn a few things from Lady Alicia. It says as much in the London Gazette."

Justin picked up the paper and searched for his book on the review page.

"Where? There is no review of my story here." He gave his uncle a questioning stare.

"Read the review for The Lost Dowry. The reviewer mentioned you as well." The publisher pointed to the paper in his hand. "The last paragraph."

The room was quiet except for the fire snapping in the grate. His uncle worked on the papers in front of him while Justin read the review.

"Anonymous likes my Captain Mallory well enough." Justin's mouth curved into an unconscious smile as he continued reading.

His amusement quickly died. He lowered his hand to his side still holding the Gazette.

"By all that is holy," he said, his Scottish brogue unmistakable in his words. "What does he mean, I need assistance with the female point of view?"

A mention in a review of her book? Not even a review of the entire story. He reeled as he re-read the paragraph and grasped the meaning. Rubbish. Learn from Lady Alicia? An absurd idea. He gave an indifferent chuckle, returned the paper to his uncle, and continued to search the basket while he seethed.

"You laugh. Read her stories. Especially her last—"

"The one with the scathing review?" Justin interrupted, not lifting his head.

"Read it, Justin, and you will understand my meaning. She portrays her female characters in a unique manner."

"How do you accept a review from someone who is ashamed to use his name, or…" Justin picked up his head and gave his uncle a questioning glance. "Do you know who wrote it?"

"I spoke with Herbert, the editor of the Gazette. Questioned him about the review. He confided one of their trusted reviewers wrote the piece."

"Could Anonymous be a competitive author?"

Would an author question a fellow writer's work publicly for their own gain? The idea was not impossible.

"No. Not at all. This was a constructive review." Uncle Isaac sat in his leather chair with an air of authority. His adamant response startled Justin.

The man protected the woman as if she were his own daughter. Justin had no intention of conducting business in such a manner when he took over the reins.

Where is that list? He didn't have time to spend all day here.

"What are you pecking around for?" His uncle pulled his chair closer to the desk.

"The titles of the books you wanted me to deliver to Mrs. Miller."

"I've sent the list to the press room and asked that the books be bundled and ready for you tomorrow. Pick them up on the press floor before you leave in the morning."

He put the papers in his hand back into the basket.

"I'm finished here. I'll see you when I return from Sommer-by-the-Sea." Justin stood and retrieved his hat from the mantel.

"You have my thanks."

"What are you thanking me for? Your request was not inconvenient. I already had plans to stay there." Justin glanced at him. The man was full of surprises today.

"Mrs. Miller has a solid business and increases her orders with us each month."

Justin inclined his head and murmured, "She's an important client and needs special care."

"True, but my gratitude extends beyond you delivering the books. Your idea to purchase a new iron press was brilliant. The men were spending more time repairing the old one than printing. The quality of the books, as well as the quantity, is much improved as well.

"I had no one to take over the company. That is, until you came to us. Your stories, your leadership, and your ideas proved to me you were the perfect person to succeed me. I decided then and there I would leave you with everything in place, the authors and updated equipment. I'm eager to see how you will grow the company."

Justin had suggested the purchase months ago. However, once his uncle approached him to be his successor, he was sure his plans had changed. Justin saw his responsibility as winding down Caulfield Publishing.

Buying a new press was not the action of a man closing his business.

No one was more surprised than he was when he met Lord Stanhope at White's. His lordship told him all about the hard bargain his uncle struck with him.

"And that's not all. Your Aunt Lavinia is making demands on my time, and I haven't yet retired. I've worked hard to make Caulfield Publishing a success. You are loyal and worthy to be my successor. I leave the business in your capable hands. Now, be off with you before I say something sentimental."

Justin hesitated a moment before he put on his hat, avoiding his uncle's stare, afraid the man would see his shameful expression.

"Have a safe trip," his uncle said. He picked up a manuscript from the stack on his desk and began to read.

He loved his uncle for his encouragement, support, and sincerity. He built a small but mighty company that was sound, from the work he produced to the income he made. This turn of events was unforeseen.

Loyal. Worthy. Capable hands.

Justin closed the door behind him. His blood turned cool as he went down the stairs. He left the building and at the corner, removed a letter from his pocket.

His uncle pushed him to be more ambitious with his writing.

"Seek out a publisher who can get you places I can't."

He could have strangled the man for sending Lane his manuscript without telling him.

The unsolicited message from William Lane Publishing informed him that he was one of two authors under consideration for the last position on their list. The message came at the right time, or so he thought. He had to find another publisher with Caulfield Publishing closing. This was the opportunity he and his uncle had spoken about months ago.

He glanced up at the office window. His uncle never planned to close the company. He walked on. What was he to do now?

About Ruth A. Casie

Ruth A Casie is a *USA Today bestselling author*. She writes historical adventures from the shores of medieval Scotland to the cobblestone streets of Regency London. Within the pages you'll discover 'edge-of-your-seat' suspense, mind boggling drama, and heart melting emotions featuring strong women and the men who deserve them. Grab your favorite cup of tea, or an ale if you prefer, and join her heroes and heroines as they race across the pages to find their happily ever after. Ruth hopes her stories are your next favorite adventures!

Things you may not know about me…

1. One year I traveled so much for my company that I filled up my passport.

2. If you know me, you'll find family names and places sprinkled in every one of my stories.

3. In researching old manuscripts, how they were made and how to translate them. I was so into it that I took a class at Stanford University.

4. I'm related to two Nobel laureates (Peace and Economics) but through in-laws and cannot make any claim on the gene pool.

5. A DNA match through Ancestry dot com has me linked to a king in Norway. Hmmm... my family (both sides) are from small towns in Eastern Europe. However, there may be a great love story here even if it isn't true!

For more information on Ruth, please join her newsletter or visit her online at
www.RuthACasie.com
Ruth@RuthACasie.com